Crimson Roses & Hidden Desire

Konstantina Priyadarshini Vasileiadou

Chennai • Bangalore

CLEVER FOX PUBLISHING
Chennai, India

Published by CLEVER FOX PUBLISHING 2024
Copyright © Konstantina Priyadarshini Vasileiadou 2024

All Rights Reserved.
ISBN: 978-93-56486-56-0

This book has been published with all reasonable efforts taken to make the material error-free after the consent of the author. No part of this book shall be used, reproduced in any manner whatsoever without written permission from the author, except in the case of brief quotations embodied in critical articles and reviews.

The Author of this book is solely responsible and liable for its content including but not limited to the views, representations, descriptions, statements, information, opinions and references ["Content"]. The Content of this book shall not constitute or be construed or deemed to reflect the opinion or expression of the Publisher or Editor. Neither the Publisher nor Editor endorse or approve the Content of this book or guarantee the reliability, accuracy or completeness of the Content published herein and do not make any representations or warranties of any kind, express or implied, including but not limited to the implied warranties of merchantability, fitness for a particular purpose. The Publisher and Editor shall not be liable whatsoever for any errors, omissions, whether such errors or omissions result from negligence, accident, or any other cause or claims for loss or damages of any kind, including without limitation, indirect or consequential loss or damage arising out of use, inability to use, or about the reliability, accuracy or sufficiency of the information contained in this.

CONTENTS

1. A Rough Start 1
2. The Flashback 5
3. The Football Team 11
4. A Mystery Savior 15
5. A New Player 20
6. The Fist Fight 26
7. A Forbidden Love 31
8. The Captain 35
9. Dating 40
10. The Trip 45
11. The Tournament 50
12. Reunion 56
13. Abusive 61
14. Soon Exams 67
15. Lessons Start 72
16. Home 78
17. Gone Wrong 82

18.	Why Me?	86
19.	Reality	93
20.	The Truth	98
21.	Help!	102
22.	Mission Rescue	107
23.	In Time	113
24.	Escape	117
25.	A Smooth Ending	122

A Rough Start

Everyone goes through dark times, don't they? That doesn't mean that life has lost its spark, does it? Sometimes the only thing that we keep in mind is, "It will get better", and we try to move on. In a big city where everyone goes unnoticed lived an invisible girl, unnoticed even by the smallest of creatures. She had her days but time changes everyone doesn't it? "Another tiring day, isn't it?" was the first thing Aisha thought as she opened her eyes in the morning. She got up and got ready for school. She thought it was just going to be an ordinary day, but little did she know……
"Good morning, mom," Aisha greeted as she went downstairs. "Finally, she is up", Aisha's mom rolled her eyes. "Darling, I hope you are better. Are your studies going well? I am worried about you, you never really talk to anyone. You know I am here for you right?" exclaimed Aisha's mother all at once; after all, she was concerned for her daughter. Aisha was on her way to school. She wanted to be excited, but she had no hopes anymore, she didn't expect anything from the day. She walked into her class and felt as if everyone was judging her. She felt tears filling up her eyes. "You're okay, you're okay, everything is gonna be okay, enough", she tried to calm herself, but nothing worked.

She went out of the classroom. She ran straight to the bathroom and burst out sobbing. She stared in the mirror seeing tears roll down one after the other. Two years had passed, and she still couldn't get over it. "Two years have passed and I am still sobbing, crying like a damned baby. Oh God how much I hate it. When is everything going to be better? When, huh!!?", She kept sobbing, invested in her monologue. She gathered herself up and went to class. The day was normal. She was in her own world and during the break walked around alone in the hopes of finally someone approaching her. Class ended and she thought to herself, "It's time I go talk to the coach." Aisha was trying to get in the school's football team and had been thinking about going for a long time. Walking to the coach's office, she was already thinking about going for championships with her team. She was thinking about making friends, going on trips and so much more. It automatically made her smile. After a long time, she was walking with hope in her eyes. She smiled and it felt like a century had passed since she had last smiled. "I am here to speak to the coach", she asked the front lady at the front office with a bright smile on her face. "Why darling any matter to discuss?" she wondered. "I wanna join the football team," Aisha replied with her eyes gleaming with glee. "Sure," the lady said, got up from her desk and led Aisha inside. "Sir I have someone who wants to join the football team," she said and smiled. "Who is the new guy?" exclaimed the coach about to get the biggest shock of his life. The receptionist chuckled, "It's not a guy but a girl." "Hello sir, I am Aisha, I am here to join the football team," Aisha said immediately, not giving the coach time to react. "She? Is this some kind of joke? You guys are kidding me, right?" The coach was shocked. Understandable as it was the first time, he had seen a girl interested in football. Aisha was kind of hurt, a bit offended and a long pause continued. "Come with me," the coach said, breaking the endless silence. The receptionist gave Aisha a warm smile and left. The coach led Aisha to a room full of sports equipment and told her to take some stuff and go outside. So she did, and while going outside, she felt excited. She wanted to prove to the coach that she was also worthy. And so the training started. Aisha ran here and there and did exactly as she was told to. "Run faster! Run! Go get the ball!" yelled the coach. Aisha ran and did her best. A little secret was that it was her first time being trained, she was new to this, but she still gave her best. At the end of the day, isn't it all about trying. The training was for one and a half hours. The time had finally ended as Aisha was soaked in sweat. "You did good for a newbie," he said coldly. If truth be told, Aisha wasn't the quite best, but the coach saw that she tried, he saw her will and was quite impressed. "Thank you, sir," Aisha said in joy. She was proud of herself. She couldn't stop smiling, which was quite unusual for her. Aisha and the coach collected the equipment and went and kept it back, "You are quite good I see, tomorrow I want you here from 3 to 4:30 to meet the rest of the team," the coach told Aisha. Okay sir, thank you for your time", Aisha said before leaving for her home. "Today I practiced alone and from tomorrow I will be with a team. I can't wait for tomorrow. Maybe I will make some friends," Aisha was shining. She went skipping home thinking how happy she would be and how everything would get better, now that she is also a part of something. She reached home and headed towards her room. She placed her bag on her room's floor and went to take a hot shower. By the time she was out of the shower it was already 06:30 pm. She heard the front door open and her mom coming in. "Mom! Mom! You won't believe what happened today." She yelled while running down the stairs in full excitement. "Aisha don't run that fast, else you will fall." Mom chuckled as she was delighted to see her daughter this happy after so many days. In detail Aisha told her mother everything not missing one single detail, "you must be tired darling eat something", said Mom while serving dinner. Aisha quickly ate and continued talking until nothing was left to say anymore. "I am glad to see you happy, baby… always stay like this," smiled Aisha's mom. "Goodnight Mother," a smile was plastered on Aisha's face before heading upstairs to her room. She lay on her bed, staring at the ceiling thinking about everything that happened that day. She was happy and excited, and for the first time she had hopes for herself. "I can't keep imagining shit ahhh….," she got up and took out her books to study. She studied at night as that was when she found her peace. She used to be such a jolly person but had changed with time. She tried studying but her focus was on a million other things. She kept her books aside and once again played numb thinking about the past. Some things are never forgotten no matter how much time passes. Sometimes even when you have a good day, thinking takes over you. Sometimes all you wish is to forget. She closed her eyes while slowly drifting to sleep.

The Flashback

*L*et me take you to the time when things were not like this.

As I said, things always change, don't they? Just 2 years ago Aisha had the life that everyone would dream of. She was the most popular girl in the entire school, everyone loved her. There was quite no one who didn't know her name. When she walked into a room, all the eyes used to fall on her. Was it her beauty? Or was it her personality? No one knew, the only thing that was sure was that she was adored by everyone who knew her. "Aisha! We are late again, the teacher is going to punish the hell out of us," said Aisha's classmate Lily worried as both were late. "Why do you worry when Aisha is here huh! Follow my lead!" said Aisha before walking in the classroom with courage as her friend silently followed. "You are late," the teacher gritted her teeth trying to control her anger. "Ma'am I understand I may be late, but I am always here in your class, and I think the most important thing for you needs to be the presence of your students. So, although I do apologize for being late, I expect you to forgive us and understand our position," Aisha said this in such a charming manner that her whole class was left stunned. Everyone admired her and she stood with pride. Sadly, her pride did not last for long as the teacher yelled "Yah! You think you can do whatever you like huh! How dare you barge in like that!?

Both of you stand with your hands up behind the class!". So, they silently went and stood with their hands up. Aisha was not a quiet kid but a naughty one, so she was used to being punished by her teachers. The class soon ended as Aisha and her friend Lily walked out of the class. "My hands feel so sore," complained Aisha to her friend. "Who told you to be stupid and give a bad speech to the teacher huh?" chuckled Lily. "Who knew that witch would get mad so easily," said Aisha as they both walked home. "Tomorrow is Saturday. So, let's meet at 9 in the morning what do you think?" asked Aisha as they were always together at the weekends. "Ah fine, I will tell Rose and Jasmine too," said Lily, knowing she had no options. " It's going to be a blast," said Aisha, before bidding goodbye to Lily and going home. She went home, ate, did her studies and of course, talked to her friends, and just like that a normal day ended. The sunshine from her window woke Aisha up. "Aisha wake up, you lazy girl…till when you going to sleep huh?" asked Aisha's mom, taking the blanket from her. "Leave me na," Aisha whined like a little kid. "Your friends are waiting outside Aisha ", said Mom. "What! It's already 9 am!? Ah," yelled Aisha before putting on some decent clothes excited to meet her friends. "Mom I am going out," Aisha yelled and ran outside to meet her friends. "Have something before you go," said Mom but it was too late she was like a flash of lighting. "Lily! Jasmine! Rose! I missed you guys so much", said Aisha jumping into their arms. "Come here, my baby I missed you more," said Jasmine who was like the mom of the group. She always took care of everyone. "Ask your baby the way she was sleeping after making plans with us," said Rose hitting Aisha's head. Rose was cold with everyone but with the girls she found peace. "I told you she would be late, didn't I?" exclaimed Lily. Lily was Aisha's classmate and the child of the group. "I am here now guys come on," Aisha whined and held Jasmine's hand and skipped in front. They went to their colony's terrace; it was their hangout spot. They felt comfortable there, they felt like they were safe there like it was their small home. That place was filled with tons of memories. "I don't want to sit down," said Aisha and pouted "Such a child! Come sit on my lap baby," said Jasmine as she sat crossed-legged down on the cement. "And what about me, huh?" said Lily while choking. "You come sit on me," said Rose and sat down. Usually, they used to sit and listen to music but today was different, their minds were filled with ideas of catastrophe. "Can we not sit and mourn I am so darn bored," Aisha whined and got up at once. "And what exactly do you plan to do huh," Lily said as she sat up. "I don't know!" exclaimed Aisha. "I agree with Aisha," said Jasmine, as she got up with the others. Everyone looked at Rose as she was the only one sitting. "You don't expect me to get up, do you?" Rose said, feeling too bored and lazy to get up. "Come on Rose," said Jasmine waiting for her to get up. "What will I do with you guys," sighed Rose as she got up and looked at them with a done expression. They walked around thinking what they should do until Jasmine noticed a ladder that led to a room on the terrace just a bit away from where they were sitting. "Let's go and try getting in that room, who knows what we discover," said Jasmine excitedly. So they did. One after the other they climbed up the ladder and reached just in front of the locked room where you had to stand before going in. To their surprise, the room was locked. They pushed and pulled with no luck. After 15 minutes of constant trying, they gave up. "We have come this far so let's just sit here," said Jasmine led up as she sat down. The girls sat down with her. Aisha sat on Jasmine's lap and so did Lily on Rose's lap.

They started talking about everything that was going on in their lives. They used to share everything. They were just like a small family. Soon they started playing some music and screaming and singing to it. They were having the time of their lives. Time flew quickly and soon they decided to go hang out somewhere else. Rose gets down first. "Can you pick me up on your back?" said Lily to Rose. "How can I say no to you?" said Rose, as Lily slipped on her back. "Me too! Me too!" said Aisha to Jasmine. Jasmine got down and told Aisha to hop on her back. Aisha jumped on Jasmine's back, but she slipped and slid on her back and fell on a water pipe. The water pipe broke and Aisha's clothes got soaked in water. Jasmine picked Aisha up. Scared, they all ran down. "What should we do now?" said Aisha panicked as it was all her fault. Jasmine hugged Aisha trying to comfort her. "Let's go tell the people of the colony otherwise they will think that we broke it," suggested Rose. Her idea was that if they told the people then they would not suspect them. They all went around trying to find someone. Soon they saw a couple of people sitting together Jasmine took the lead and said, "The pipe at the terrace broke and there is water everywhere." "You guys broke it, didn't you?" exclaimed an old guy who was sitting with the others. "No! If we had done it, we wouldn't have come and told you." Rose was quick to respond and they bought that lie! A few of them went to check the pipe as the girls unnoticed left from there. They went and sat on a bench still in a bit of a shock at what had happened. "Thank god Rose made up that lie, or I cannot imagine what would have happened," said Lily while sobbing on Aisha's back who was still in a bit of a shock on what had just happened. Ten minutes had passed and they all had calmed down a bit. Just as they thought that they had gotten away with it, they saw a man coming towards them. He was old, around his mid 60's. His eyes were filled with anger. He went near them and started yelling at them at the top of his lungs, "How dare you guys break the pipe huh!? Do you even know how much money it costs?" The girls were scared; they didn't know how to react. "Who is this random bozo yelling at us?" thought Aisha and looked at the girls who were all horrified.

"We didn't," stuttered Jasmine. "No, you did! Don't lie to me. I heard you guys. Do you know that because of you, people won't have water in their house, huh! " He kept yelling for another 15 mins before leaving. They were scared and didn't know how to react. "How dare he yell at us like that huh, how dare he?" said Jasmine. Aisha noticed tears in Jasmine's eyes and rubbed her back. "I don't think we should go home now. I believe they would have already told our parents," said Rose. "What about lunch, I am hungry," said Aisha while rubbing her tummy. "You care about food right now!" said Rose hitting Aisha on her head. "Don't fight, I have some money. For now, let's just go from here," said Lily as they all got up and went to a nearby park. Lily got them some food and they spent their day there. Soon it was time to go home. They got up and had almost forgotten what had happened before. Laughing and giggling, they went to drop Lily at her house as it was the closest. All the laughter and giggles vanished as they saw their parents waiting for them. As usual, they were all put in a room and yelled at. After about an hour of scolding and taunting they all went home. Aisha went to bed a bit tired from all the yelling but surprisingly she was happy. Even though she got into trouble, she was with her friends. It was a memory she would always remember. She closed her eyes, drifting in a sweet sleep. She had no idea that this night was the last night that she would sleep peacefully. The next day passed peacefully. Lily, Rose, Jasmine, and Aisha met up in the morning and hung out till the evening. The girls gathered up with some of the boys in their colony and started playing dodgeball. Roughly 20 minutes later Aisha's mom called her home. It was unusual and to be honest she was a little scared. She went home and her mom sat her down and said, "We will have to shift." Aisha felt like her whole world came crashing down. "What! Why? No Mom this can't happen," Aisha didn't want to accept this. "My job got a transfer and there is nothing I can do about it," Aisha's mom got up and patted Aisha on her back, and left. Aisha felt lost, she didn't know how to react, she didn't even want to go back to her friends. How would she tell them? What would they think? Tears filled her eyes as she lay hugging her pillow for some comfort. She cried herself to sleep that night. The days passed in the blink of an eye. The day came when she had to leave. "Take care of yourself for me, okay baby?" said Jasmine, wiping Aisha's tears. She hugged everyone. With the corner of her eye, she noticed Rose crying for the first time. Aisha went up to Rose and hugged her. "Don't cry Rose I hate seeing you like this". "I am not crying," said Rose wiping her tears. "Group hug!" yelled Lily and rushed to them and hugged them. "What are you waiting for?" said Aisha to Jasmine as they all had a last group hug. You might think that after that they kept in touch, but Jasmine, Rose, and Lily all cut Aisha off. They blamed her because the group broke. Aisha was torn apart as she didn't make any new friends and a part of her will always be in them no matter what.

The Football Team

Aisha woke up crying, she remembered everything. Losing her friends, getting blamed, having no one, it all came to her mind. "I couldn't believe it how could so much change in 2 years, just how I always knew I had issues but this happening? I am done, done with everyone. I want to disappear. I wish I never existed. How could I let something like this happen?" She laid in her bed, sobbing, feeling nothing but grief and sorrow. She always said 'don't cry over spilt milk' but this milk had fallen on her and it was burning hot. She gathered herself up and got ready. "Mom, I am leaving," uttered Aisha before walking out the door. "But breakfast," her mom was cut off by the sound of the door shutting. Aisha went and sat in her class. "Have you heard there is a new member joining the football team?" "Damn no, hope he is good". She overheard 2 students talking. Suddenly, she was filled with excitement. She couldn't wait to go to her first practice with the others. All her sadness disappeared, and excitement took over her. She couldn't wait to go to her football lessons today. It was the third period. Another 4 hours to go. Aisha was already exhausted. Suddenly an idea popped up in her head. As you might have guessed, she planned to bunk her class. "Ma'am my stomach hurts," she said getting up as she was quickly sent to the nurse. "Should we call your mom?" the nurse asked, "No, no she must be at work. Let me go," pleaded Aisha with the sweetest little eyes ever. "Okay but this is the first and the last time," said the nurse and gave her a slip to go. She left quickly without saying anything so no one got suspicious. Aisha had some money on her, so she decided to go and buy some football equipment. "It's a good thing I carry money with me, or I would have been bored, " thought Aisha, as she walked in the sports shop. The sports shop was huge. It was filled with all kinds of equipment. "Woah!" exclaimed Aisha as she walked around in amazement.

She roamed around, forgetting what she was there for. "Aisha, focus, you need to buy things," she said, getting her mind on track and quickly going to the football aisle. There were all kinds of stuff. Aisha didn't waste a minute more and bought all that she needed. She was so happy but had spent so much, though she didn't care. She was happy and so excited to go. Soon the time came. Aisha went to school changed and was making her hair. The school had ended and her class was about to start. As soon as she saw the time, she ran to the field. On the field there were 12 boys standing in line with their hands on their backs. "Sorry sir I am late," said Aisha, as she went and stood near the coach. "It's fine," said the coach and soon continued, "Guys, this is Aisha. She is going to be your new teammate as there is no girl's team at our school, ok? I hope you all will accept her and treat her well, and boys no mischief!" Aisha felt nervous but still smiled. She didn't want to give them a bad impression. The coach told them to go warm up, and left for a while. One of the guys went up to Aisha and pushed her down as another went and stood in front of her. "Little girl, stay within your limits and don't you dare try to boss us around. If you open your mouth to anyone, I will make sure you pay for it," he roared. It was Alex, the school bully. Everyone feared him. Everyone used to hide when he walked down a corridor. Strong, tall, and brown hair, Alex was never good news. Alex had a best friend, Sid. The boy who pushed Aisha down. He was always accompanying Alex in whatever he did whether good or bad, but I think we both know nothing he did was good. All the boys laughed at Aisha as she was stunned. She got up slowly and continued warming up. The class continued and Alex kept picking on Aisha. No one said anything. The coach wasn't around and none of the boys said anything as they were afraid of Alex. The class ended and Aisha couldn't wait to go home. She went back home and went straight to her room. She threw everything she had bought in the corner of the room and broke down crying. "Why god why? Why me, what have I done?" she sobbed. "I just wanted to make some damn friends is that too much to ask. Is having hope such a bad thing? For once I had expectations and they all got ruined. Why can't anyone be happy with my happiness?"

Her room was filled with cries and sobs. Exhausted from the tears rolling down her bright red cheeks, she slowly got up and placed her numb body on her pillow soft mattress and soon drifted off to the only place that would never hurt her, her dreamland. As the moon rose high the bright moonlight showered upon her soft paper skin. The dried tears on her cheeks looked like small raindrops, her pillow soaked with tears, her hair falling on her face like a beautiful curtain covering a window. The pain she was feeling was unbearable; sometimes we never know what a person is going through until we are put in their place, right? The morning came along as Aisha got up for another tiring day. She was still tired from all the tears that were shed yesterday. She got herself up and dragged herself to school. She was tired of having hope after yesterday's incident. The class started as she was in her world, daydreaming about a better place somewhere far away from the harsh reality she was living in. Soon, school ended, and it was time for her football lessons. She went to the restroom and got dressed. She tied her in a bun and stared at herself in the mirror. "You are strong, you can do this," this phrase kept circling in her mind, trying to muster up the energy to face her hell. On the thought of being bullied again her lower lip quivered as tears filled up her eyes. She wiped her tears and got herself together as she walked to the field. Everyone was in a line and Aisha went and joined them. As usual, the coach told them to start warming up and left again for some paperwork. They were running in the field warming themselves up as Alex got to it again. "Hey girl you back today again huh!" he softly yelled, as he walked towards her intimidatingly. "Stay away!" exclaimed Aisha. "Sid, are you looking at this? Little girlie is talking back," chuckled Alex, pushing Aisha to the ground. Everyone burst out laughing at her. "Leave her alone!" a deep raspy voice roared from behind…

A Mystery Savior

Shivers ran down her spine. She didn't know who was behind her, nor did she recognize his voice. "I don't have time for this," scoffed Alex, as he walked away. Aisha slowly got up and turned around to thank her mystery savior. As she turned around, her mouth was left hanging open. A guy with black hair and deep brown eyes stood in front of her. He was tall, around six feet, and had a strong, bulky body. "Are you okay?" his deep voice yet again sent shivers down her spine. He softly held her arm, turned her around and dusted the grass off her back. Aisha snapped back to reality. "Y-yea..T..thank you," she stuttered still in a slight shock. "It's nothing, take care hmmm?" the boy said. Aisha nodded, and both continued warming up with the rest of the team. The entire time no one dared to say anything to Aisha, scared that the dark-haired boy would expose them to the coach. Time flew by and everything went well. Soon they were dismissed. On the way back home, Aisha's mind was filled with all kinds of thoughts. "Who was he? Why did he help me?" her mind was racing. Suddenly it hit her, she hadn't even asked for his name! '"Aisha! You are such a dumbass!" she thought before walking back home. So, who was he? The dark-haired boy was named Ryle. A good-hearted but abused kid. His Mom 'left' him when he was young, and his dad was a drunkard. Music was his getaway, he used to stay out trying to escape this nightmare called life. He was sweet and kind to everyone but mostly stayed alone. He enjoyed his own company and did not care about what anyone said. He did not have the most ideal childhood and was beaten almost every day by his father. That made him strong though, not physically but mentally. The boy didn't want to go home for understandable reasons, so he took out his headphones and plugged them into his phone. Jamming to music, he walked to a building's terrace and sat there looking at the ground. It was night and the city was slowing with lights, the cars looked tiny, and the moon was high up in the sky. The cold wind blew on his face as he closed his eyes.

"I a-am, s-sorry!" stuttered 5-year-old Ryle knowing what was coming for him. "You are sorry!" yelled the monstrous man in front of him. "I am going to make sure you are sorry by the end of this!" he yelled again, as he slid his belt out of the hoops. The room was filled with banging noises. What was the kid's fault? He had just dropped a damn beer bottle. "I am sorry I learned my lesson," cried the small kid, begging the man to stop, his body filling with bruises. Ryles eyes shot open, remembering all that he endured since he was a young kid. Flashbacks hurt, don't they? The thing that hurts the most is that you can't change anything about them, you can't change anything about the past, can you? He quickly wiped his already wet eyes and looked back down at the shining city. From the corner of his eye, he noticed a girl standing on the terrace of the next building. He recognized her. He jumped onto the nearby terrace and crept up behind her. He stopped his music and quickly put his hands on her mouth to prevent her from screaming. "Don't scream, it's me". Ryle said in a low tone. Aisha turned around shocked to see him. "What are you doing here?" she wondered aloud. "Saw you from my terrace and dropped by," he explained. "Then stay," Aisha said, standing near him as they both looked down admiring the beauty of the might. "I didn't get your name," Aisha said awkwardly. "How rude of me, I am Ryle," said the dark-haired boy. "Aisha. Nice to meet you," she said and extended her hand. They shook hands but from the corner of her eye, she noticed a dark red bruise on his hand. She grabbed his arm and pulled up his sleeve revealing bruises all over his hand. "Ryle, how did this happen?" she asked, shocked by what she saw. "I am fine," Ryle said coldly and pulled back his arm. "Ok, don't tell me but come inside let me clean that up for you I am home alone so don't worry, "She said as she softly held his arm and took him inside. Ryle stayed silent not knowing what to say. Aisha took out a first aid kit and placed it on the bed next to Ryle. "Roll up your sleeve!" She ordered and to her surprise, he listened. "This will hurt a bit," she said and started cleaning up his wounds. The hurt boy clenched onto the bed sheets, feeling his wounds burn by the touch of the medicine. The boy teared up. "It hurts," he whined, almost letting a tear escape his eye. "Shhhh, it's over now," she patted the bloody cotton on his wounds. She went and placed the kit back in its place and got out some bandages. "I will just bandage it up and it will be over hmm?" She said in a soft tone as she started bandaging his hand. "Thanks," Ryle murmured while admiring the girl who was bandaging his arm. "Why are you thanking me? I should be the one saying thanks. If it wasn't for you Alex would have beaten me up," said Aisha, making eye contact. "If he lays a finger on you, I will rip his fucking arms off," Ryle gritted his teeth. Aisha felt flattered. No one ever cared so much about her. She stared into his deep brown eyes. It feels good when a person cares about you, doesn't it? Especially when you need it the most. Suddenly they heard the front door open. "Aisha! I am home". "Run, run, run!" Aisha yelled softly as she grabbed Ryle's hand, dragging him to the terrace. "Take care," said Ryle, before jumping onto the nearby terrace and disappearing into the deep night. The boy walked home, not understanding what he was feeling. He looked at his arm which was bandaged now. He lived in a huge house, left for him by his mom. His dad was drunk on the couch, as usual. "Where were you?" his dad yelled as Ryle walked in the door. "Out," the boy replied coldly. His father struck his face. Ryle's eyes fumed with rage. He didn't respond nor looked at his father. After all these years of continuous torture, Ryle didn't care anymore. The boy looked up at his father. "I am disappointed," he sighed as he went to his room, locking it from the inside. The boy changed and lay on the bed, staring at the ceiling. "I wish momma was here," he sighed as he softly turned to his side and fell asleep. Life is a crazy thing, isn't it? It's never all good, never all bad, the only thing we know or perhaps should know is that no matter what we need to keep moving forward. Aisha was awake thinking about the boy. "What were those bruises on his arm? Is it the doing of Alex? Was he ok? Why was he so sweet? Does he care? Are we friends now?" her mind was filled with all kinds of thoughts. She fell asleep thinking about the mysterious boy. The sun rose high as Aisha had just woken up, Ryle on the other hand was out for a jog. "Morning Mom," greeted Aisha as she walked down the stairs. "Morning my early riser," said her mother and gave her a sandwich. "Mom, I am going to be late, see ya!" Aisha grabbed the sandwich and left for school. On the way, she saw Ryle. "Ryle! Wait up!" She yelled and went and stood beside him. "Morning Aisha," the brown-eyed boy smiled. "How are you? Do your wounds hurt? You slept well?" She threw in the questions. "I am fine now don't worry, I even slept well," Ryle chuckled, admiring her cuteness. They walked together to their classes. "I will be going now, if you need anything, you know where to find me," Ryle said with a warm smile. Aisha hugged him tightly. "Thank you," she whispered and went to her class. Ryle was shocked. He hadn't been hugged since his mom died. A small smile crept up on his lips as he walked into his class. Hours passed and now it was time for their football class. The well-built boy went and stood covered with bandages. No one dared to say anything about it.

Ryle was strong and almost everyone feared him. Aisha came and stood beside him. He made her feel safe, she knew that as long as he was with her, nobody could hurt her. "You need someone to protect you now, huh?" mocked Alex and everyone laughed. "Cut it out, Alex. You better go bully someone else, we have no interest in hearing your blabbering," Ryle said with a Poker face. Alex walked intimidatedly towards Aisha with fuming eyes. Ryle grabbed Aisha's hand and put her behind him. "Stay away from her," Ryle said in a deep tone, hiding Aisha behind him who clenched his shirt tightly. "Boys cut it off!" roared the coach as both boys went back in the line. "I am saddened to tell you that many members are leaving the team. To fix that problem I have gotten us a new player," said the coach with a bright smile on his face. As the boy showed himself, Aisha's mouth dropped to the ground. "I want you all to welcome Skye".

A New Player

A tall blonde guy with bright blue eyes walked out in front of them. He looked like he had come out of a movie. "Hey everyone, I am Skye," he said as he smiled brightly. Everyone was charmed, even Alex was charmed by the blonde's behavior. Training started; Aisha was lost in the Blonde's sky-blue eyes. "Someone has a crush,", Ryle teased Aisha. "Shut up!" Aisha blushed and her face turned red. Aisha saw that Skye was getting along with Alex and that scared her a bit. "Ryler...," "Yes?", "Skye is being too close to Alex, and I don't like it," Aisha said and pouted like a kid. "Don't worry must be just a friendly talk, and what's up with the nicknames?" chuckled Ryle. "I like the name Ryler, It's Sweet so I will call you that" said Aisha. "As you wish," laughed Ryle as they continued their practice. Soon when class ended Ryle decided to walk Aisha home. "I hope Alex and Skye don't team up against me," said Aisha in a low tone. "He is not that type of a person dummy, don't worry," comforted Ryle. "Hey!" They heard a voice behind them. Both turned around to see Skye. "I hope I am not interrupting anything," said the blonde (Skye) as he started walking with them. "Not at all. You are welcome, new boy", chuckled Ryle. "You both seem good, but I didn't quite catch your names," said Skye, wanting to know more about the girl and the dark-haired boy. "I am Ryle, and this is Aisha," Ryle spoke up because Aisha was blushing, completely red not being able to talk. "Nice meeting you both," Skye smiled softly. The trio kept talking and surprisingly got along. Soon the boys dropped Aisha home and were left together alone. "Stay away from Alex he is not as good as he may seem," warned Ryle not wanting the blonde to get in trouble. "I know but don't worry I've got a better trio now," chuckled Skye. "Nice knowing you man!" said Ryle, as he shook the blonde's hand and went towards his house. Skye was left all alone. Everyone has a dark side, don't they? You must be wondering what was Skye's back story. What was he hiding behind that charming smile? Skye was from a rich family; both his parents owned a big company and were always away at work. Skye was supposed to be 'the perfect child' but he had his little mind. Skye was a creative little kid who never got a chance to express himself. 'The perfect child' in reality was 'the neglected one'. Skye reached home and walked through the door in hopes someone was there. "Mom! I am home," he called out as he walked through the front and into the kitchen in search of his mother. "I am busy Skye, can't you see?" she yelled back. The blonde wasn't surprised but disappointed as he walked to his room upstairs. He put his bag down and went for a quick shower. Changed and bathed, Skye sat on his bed studying. He was expected to be good at everything from sports to studies. "Skye! Come down my boy," yelled Skye's dad from downstairs. A small smile crept up on the boy's face. His dad was never that sweet at home. The blonde ran down excited to greet his father. The boy's eyes, which were filled with love, soon turned into hatred and disgust as soon as he saw his father. Behind his father stood a reporter. As Skye's family was wealthy reporters and interviewers used to come and go now and then. The blue-eyed boy put a fake smile on his face and came down. "Hello father," he greeted and sat down on the couch with the other adults. The adults talked about things that Skye didn't care about, so he was just in his world. He couldn't care less about his parent's business affairs. Soon the reporter left as Skye's smile soon turned into a fit of anger. "Why Dad!" The boy banged his hands on the table and with a jerk got up. "Why what, Skye?" asked his father as he took out a cigarette and started smoking. "Why do you always have to pretend we are a happy family in front of others when in reality we are like this! I am so tired of pretending. I hate it so much, why can't you just lo-" Skye was cut off by a tight slap on his left cheek. "Watch your tone, Skye," his dad scoffed. Skye felt angered as rage took over him and he ran to his room locking it. His parents never cared. As a young kid, he used to feel neglected but now he simply didn't care. He was disappointed in himself that he even had hopes that his father would care. He rolled his eyes and lay numb on his bed. Meanwhile, when Ryle went home, he was greeted by his drunk dad. Ryle sighed and put down his bag. "Dad put down the bottle," said Ryle in hopes of fixing his dad's situation. "What do you care, huh!?" said his dad as he slapped Ryle. Ryle didn't react; he was used to getting beaten. Ryle was weak, he didn't have the energy to do or say anything now. The monster pushed the dark-haired boy to the ground. Of course, it wasn't the first time Ryle was getting beaten but the poor boy felt so fed up with everything and everyone that he didn't react even a bit. The man unbuckled his belt and started beating the boy mercilessly. Ryle didn't react, just flinched now and then. His body slowly started filling up with bruises, and the pain soon turned unbearable. But not a sign of pain could be seen on Ryle's face. The boy's body was aching, and he just crouched down in a ball, he didn't even try to protect himself. His dad didn't slow down a bit seeing the boy in pain. About an hour passed and soon his dad got tired, and the belt dropped down. His dad looked at the bruised boy, "I wish you were never born! It's your fault your mom died." These words hit Ryle like a knife in his heart. Tears filled up his eyes. He could think of only one phrase 'Hold your horses'. Ryle had been beaten since he was a kid so whenever he wanted to cry, he used to say, 'Hold your horses'. It meant that he needed to hold back his tears and when he was alone at night, he let his tears out on his pillow. Ryle got up and without saying anything he just left. He went to his usual spot, the nearby buildings terrace. His eyes were still filled with tears as his father's words kept repeating in his head. "Is it my fault momma died? Do I really deserve to be dead?" His mind was filled with negative thoughts. He couldn't help but blame himself. He couldn't take it any longer, his back slammed against the terrace wall, and he burst into tears. The boy felt limp on the terrace floor, warm tears rushing down his cold yet dried-up cheeks. Coming out to the balcony Aisha heard sobs. She got worried, "Who is crying at this hour?" She was a bit shocked and tried to find the source of the painful sobs. Looking over, she saw her savior, Ryle. Without wasting a minute, Aisha jumped on the nearby terrace. "Ryle!" she said and sat down to his level hugging him and seeing the bruises on his arms. His skin was peeling, his bruises were now open wounds that bled. Ryle didn't have the strength to say or explain anything. The dark-haired boy fell limp in her embrace as all the pain he had been holding inside of him was let go in the form of tears and occasional sobs that escaped his mouth. "Shhh, I am here don't worry you are not alone," Aisha comforted as she pulled him closer to her. She couldn't see the guy who had saved her, the guy who stood for her in so much pain. Her heart ached more than his, her heart clenched with every tear that rolled down his eye. "Why Aisha why! Why do I suffer? Why couldn't I be normal like everyone else! WHY!?" the boy spoke in between his sobs. Who could blame him for being this vulnerable? Aisha rubbed his back in a desperate condition to comfort him. She pulled him closer to her chest, placing his head near her heart so he could hear her heartbeat. The boy calmed down after a while. "Feeling better?" she asked in a comforting tone as the boy softly nodded. "Come to my room, my mom's asleep," She held his hand and took him to her room. The boy sat on her bed still sniffing and wiping his dried tears from the breakdown he just had. Aisha bought the first aid kit again just like yesterday. "Take off your shirt," she demanded. "W-why... no", he didn't want her to see his bruises. "I don't want to hurt you Ryler, I can't see you like this. Please let me help," she said and caressed the black-haired boy's hair. The boy innocently nodded and took off his shirt. His fine-muscled body was filled with red bruises that looked like they could bleed at any time now. Her heart shattered in a million pieces seeing him in that state. "Turn around", she said as he listened. His back was the same, bruised up. "Brace yourself," She warned and started cleaning his wounds. The boy hissed to the ointment touching his wounds. "Shhh you can hold my hand", Aisha said and extended her hand as he quickly held it tightly. She cleaned him up and bandaged him. "Feeling better?" She smiled. "Much better," Ryle smiled back at her. "Care to tell me how it happened Ryler? You know I am always here for you right?" Aisha said she was worried for him. Ryle explained to her everything about his abusive dad and his mom dying. He wanted to feel vulnerable, and she heard him out and made him feel safe.

"I am always here, Ryler," She comforted him. "Thanks, Aisha, means a lot. I need to get home now it's late", said Ryle as he got up. "Go home safe, if you need me, you can always come over, okay?" Aisha just wanted him to stay safe. Ryle nodded as he headed home.

The Fist Fight

The moonlight shone bright in the dark lonely streets. Ryle walked in dark silence, his only light being the moon above his head. He was happy. Was it his time with Aisha? Was it the fact that his wounds didn't hurt anymore? He didn't care; he was glad that he had a soft smile on his face. Ryle went home and ignoring the mess, he walked into his room. He dimmed the lights and stared at the ceiling. At that moment, life seemed pretty, he closed his eyes feeling grateful for everything he had.

Headphones plugged in, music blasting in his ears, Skye was dancing in his room. He had no care for anyone. Jumping on his bed listening to rock music, he loved it. Someone knocked on his door, but he couldn't hear it. "Skye?" a soft voice asked before opening the door. Skye noticed his door opening and took off his headphones, "Eleonora?" People are weird, aren't they? Just when you think no one cares about you, someone always shows up. I believe you are never lonely, there is always someone who wants to be there for you, who loves you. Eleonora was Skye's younger sister, the only one in his family who loved him and cared for him. "Skye, I brought you some food. You haven't eaten anything since morning," she said and sat on Skye's bed. "I don't want to eat, Eleonora, I don't have an appetite," said the boy, sitting down cross-legged on his bed. "I don't care Skye! Eat up,"

She started feeding him. Skye chuckled at her words but started eating. Eleonora loved Skye, he was always there for her, so she wanted to do the same. After she fed Skye, she got up but before leaving turned to him and said, "Ignore dad, he is not worth your time. Focus on yourself, don't give a damn about others, I love you." She smiled and left. Skye felt touched. His little sister had grown up. The boy sat on his bed using his phone. It was almost 2 am but there was no sign of sleep in his eyes. He stayed thinking about the one he loved… The one he went to see today. Thinking about the one you love is a beautiful thing. There was no doubt, Skye was in love. Skye had been in love for a long time now. Though he never had the guts to say it. He got one step closer to the person he adored the most. Skye closed his eyes imagining fake scenarios in his head. He slowly drifted into a sweet wonderland, where love was true. Sadly, in the morning he had to wake up to a rude and mean reality. Sometimes you ask yourself why are people like this, why don't people change, and to be honest, in my knowledge, there is no answer.

As the sunshine hit her face, her sweet little eyes opened. Aisha sat up on her bed. Today she didn't want to get up. Her eyebrows clenched together trying to forget a nightmare that she had last night. Tears filled her eyes as she laid back down hugging her pillow. She took her phone and checked the time. "Shoot! I am late," she shot up, grabbed her bag and ran to school. Ryle saw her on the way. "Looking good in your night suit," he chuckled. "Shut up," she pouted "I thought I was late," Ryle laughed at her silliness though he thought she looked cute. They went to their classes and Ryle couldn't stop thinking about Aisha, how yesterday she had taken care of him, supported him, and most importantly, did not judge him. Meanwhile, the school's sweetheart was the best student. Always answering the questions, he had perfect grades. As usual, the class ended and all three of them met up. Ryle and Skye were in a deep conversation about their common beliefs about how a team captain should be. Aisha was lost in Skye's ocean eyes; she indeed had a small little crush. Soon Alex came and started warming up. "You're late!" said Skye in a slightly irritated tone. This took Alex by surprise. Till yesterday Skye and Alex were on good terms, so why the hell was he talking to him like that? "What do you care?" replied Alex in an intimidating tone. Skye stopped warming up and walked up to Alex as Alex did the same. The heat was intense, and everyone's gaze turned tp the two boys. "Guys stop," said Aisha trying to calm down the situation. "Who the hell asked you to open your mouth?" said Alex in an irritating tone. "Don't talk to her like that!" a hard punch landed on Alex's face. Aisha was shocked but even more astonished was Ryle. Skye was never a violent person, at least he didn't seem like one. It took no time for the boys to get into a fistfight. Soon Skye's nose started bleeding and as soon as the coach saw the boys, he rushed and broke them off. "Principal's office now!" yelled the coach, disappointed in the boys. "And you all continue. I will be back later." Skye and Alex were taken to the principal's office. The boys kept glaring at each other Alex was used to being in trouble, but it was Skye's first time being there. Surprisingly, he wasn't nervous when they called his parents. Was it the fact that he didn't care about them or was it just his fuming rage, he didn't know, and he didn't care. Soon his parents came into the office and went to talk to the principal. Both had a look of disappointment on their face, but Skye couldn't care less. In no time, Eleonora walked in. She was the only one who had a worried look on her face. She walked up to Skye and sat on her knees in front of him cupping his cheeks. "Are you okay? Does it hurt?" asked the girl with tears in her eyes. Skye's heart broke into a million pieces seeing her like that. The blond nodded and wiped her tears. Skye was feeling guilty as he was the cause of his sister's tears. "It's okay El. I am okay. I am not that hurt don't cry," Skye hugged her. "Kids, get up, we are going home," there was Skye's dad to ruin the moment. Skye's parents walked to their car as the kids followed. Eleonora held Skye's hand to make him feel better. The ride home was silent, no one said anything. Skye's father seemed calm, but Skye knew that this was calm before the storm. As soon as they reached, Skye's dad got out of the car, harshly grabbed Skye's arm, and pulled him out of the car. He was dragged inside the house so roughly that it made Eleonora let go of Skye's hand. Skye's dad pushed Skye onto the couch "Are you in your right mind?! Do you know that you could have ruined our entire reputation!" Skye's dad yelled enraged. Skye's mom and Eleonora just stared. Eleonora could not do anything and that broke her heart. Skye was torn, instead of caring about if he was well his dad cared about his reputation. What a selfish bastard. Skye wanted to say but he knew it would cause a bigger mess and didn't want to hurt his sister. "Are you even listening!?" yelled Skye's mom. "I can't even look at you, this time you are forgiven but don't you dare do it again. Go to your room now," said Skye's dad and rubbed his temples. Skye silently went to his room without saying a word. "Will he be, okay?" asked Aisha to Ryle. "I hope so," replied the dark-haired boy as they walked home together. "He stood up for me," Aisha smiled to herself. "You must be glad, eh?" Ryle teased her. knowing she now liked Skye. "I told you he would like you!" "But I feel guilty, it's my fault he is in trouble," said Aisha and pouted. "Don't overthink, it he will be okay I promise," Ryle said and pecked Aisha on the forehead and went inside his home.

Skye took a shower and lay on his bed tired. He didn't have dinner and he knew that Eleonora wasn't allowed to see him. Skye was guilty of leaving his lover behind back at the school. Skye heard his parents talking downstairs and he heard his name. Interested, he put his ear on his door to eavesdrop. "This boy will cause us problems one day. I swear to God not having a kid would have been so much better," he heard his mom say. "Don't worry, we will find a way to tame him. Where he will go?" his dad replied. Skye didn't want to hear anymore. He felt worthless as hell. Why couldn't his parents accept him the way he is, why couldn't they be normal like all the others? Skye grabbed his phone and wrote a text. He went to his balcony and looked down. He climbed over the railing and closed his eyes. 3…2… 1" and he jumped. Silence filled the night. "Boom!" He fell on some bushes and looked around; he quickly got up and ran out of his backyard. Skye had sneaked out. He ran to the school field and sat there. He stared into the empty darkness feeling absolutely nothing. Suddenly he felt a soft tap on his shoulder. With a jerk, Skye turned around and there standing was… Alex. Alex harshly grabbed Skye's arm and pulled him up, glaring at him. They both shared a moment of silence. Alex kept staring into the blondes' eyes with rage. Skye was trembling now. Alex grabbed Skye, tightly squeezing his arm and smashed his lips onto Skye's.

A Forbidden Love

The two boys kissed finally after a long time Skye cupped Alex's cheeks deepening the kiss. Only a few days had passed since they held each other but it felt like centuries. After a while, Alex broke the kiss and scanned Skye's face, "Are you okay? Why were you acting weird today? Did you get into any trouble at home?" Alex was worried about Skye; though mad, Alex still cared about the blonde boy, at the end of the day he was his lover. "I am fine Alex," Skye hugged him. "Ryle and Aisha started getting suspicious about why I was getting close to you," Skye sighed. "I didn't mean to hurt you, I did it for us I don't want anything to happen to us at any cost. I am so-". "Shhh I understand Skyllar you don't need to explain yourself to me." Alex comforted Skye. Skye had missed Alex's soft embrace. The boys sat down as Skye sort on Alex's lap.

They cuddled in each other's embrace. Both boys lacked affection and that is what led them to each other. Only a year had passed since they met but it felt like centuries since they had known each other. The two lovers gazed up at the stars embracing their Forbidden love. It was only a year ago that Alex kept up with his attitude. The boy was bullied when he was young so when he changed schools, he quickly found Sid and became a bully. What Alex did was wrong, but it was his defense tactic. It was just another normal day for Alex, but little did he know he would be discovering a secret that even he had kept from himself. Alex walked around with Sid picking on people.

Alex had heard about Skye and how he was from a perfect family, the perfect child, and decided to go pick on him. Alex and Sid walked up to Skye. "Hey! Blonde boy!" Alex called out as Skye turned around. Those two bright blue eyes shone through Alex's soul. He felt like he had seen the most beautiful being that he had ever laid eyes on. Alex came back to reality as soon as Sid said, "There you are pretty blonde boy!" Alex grabbed Skye by the collar and picked him up. Skye's feet could barely touch the ground. Alex held Skye and banged his hand on the locker just beside Skye's head. "L...let m...me go...," stuttered Skye. "Awww you trying to say something?" Sid teased as tears filled up Skye's eyes. Alex kept hitting the locker beside Skye's head. Tears ran down the blonde's eyes as he kept flinching at the loud sound just beside his ear. Alex wanted to stop for the first time he felt guilty. He pitied the boy. After about fifteen minutes Alex let Skye down and without saying anything walked off with Sid. The day passed but Alex couldn't get the blue-eyed boy out of his mind. It was a weird feeling in his chest. He never felt like that before. As class ended Alex started walking alone towards his home. He was thinking about his day, about Skye. Out of nowhere, he heard a sound. It was like a little kid crying. Though Alex was a bully, he loved kids. He walked towards the sound that led to a small park and to no one's surprise he saw Skye. Guilt took over Alex's body; he walked up to Skye and sat near him, "Skye?" Skye looked at him with tears filled his eyes but as soon as he looked at Alex fear took over him. "Please don't hurt me," the blond covered his arms for protection. "I am not going to hurt you Skye," said Alex in a guilty tone. "You know my name," said the blonde looking in his eyes tears still rolling. Every tear that rolled down Skye's eyes made Alex's heart clench. "I do, now don't cry, I am sorry," Alex couldn't recognize himself. He never thought he would apologize for anything but with Skye it was different. Wasting no moment, Skye lunged at him and hugged him. "It's okay I forgive you." Alex was shocked but didn't realize when a small smile crept up on his face. Alex patted the blond's back. They both soon started talking and figured that surprisingly they had many things in common. The boys got along well but kept it a secret. They used to meet every day after school and soon turned into good friends. It all happened so quickly that they didn't realize when their friendship turned into love. They knew everything about each other so much that they could predict every move the other one made. That was their sweet little love story. Back to the present, the boys lay there admiring the stars. After a hard day this was all, they needed, being snuggled up with the one they loved the most. Hours passed like seconds when they were with each other and soon it was time to end their beautiful night. Alex turned his head towards his ocean-eyed lover. "Baby, it's time. You know that right?" said the boy, as he caressed his lovers light blonde hair. "I don't want to leave, this night is so mesmerizing I don't want it to end," Skye was now teary. "I know baby boy, but all good things come to an end right," Alex comforted. "Why is being without you so hard? I hate it! Everyone seems so mean and rude, no one accepts me for who I am. I put a fake face on so that everyone is happy. With you, I can be open. But why is our time so limited? I wish to not hide myself anymore, us anymore," Skye sobbed in Alex's arms. Alex was left speechless, he knew that Skye wasn't wrong, he had a reason to be sad. "Shhh don't cry my love" Alex pulled Skye onto his lap rubbing his back. "One day this night more will have our happily ever after." Alex picked up Skye and pecked his forehead. "Be strong baby boy," Alex said as Skye gave him a warm smile. Meanwhile, Ryle was awake at midnight as his mind was racing with a million thoughts. He couldn't stop thinking about Aisha, how she was, all he wanted, all he cared about. Suddenly it hit him, she didn't love him, she wanted Skye. The realization hit him like a truck at full speed. His wounds still hurt from the beating but now his heart ached more. He liked Skye and surprisingly thought that Skye and Aisha looked good together. Without realizing, tears filled the dark-haired boy's eyes and as soon as a tear rolled down his cheek, he wiped it off aggressively. He rubbed his eyes so hard that they turned red. The poor boy closed his eyes but deep down he knew, "No matter how much I tried she would never be mine…"

The Captain

The night rolled by in the blink of an eye. The sun rose high as the 3 torn-apart lovers woke up. Love is weird, I believe. What do you do when the person you love doesn't love you back? Do you stop loving them? Is it that easy? Ryle woke up a bit low for obvious reasons. He skipped school and the boy was in no mood to see anyone. Aisha, sitting in her class, was worried about Ryle. "Is he in trouble? I don't know where he is, I haven't seen him since the morning." Negative thoughts filled her mind. It was noon and the football team united in the field. Aisha saw Ryle talking to Skye and rushed over to the two boys. "Ryle! Where were you? I was worried the whole damn day," Aisha said and hugged Ryle. Aisha's heart was racing as she was tensed, so much so that Ryle could feel her heart beating. He hugged her back. "I just wasn't in a mood to come today; don't worry I am fine," said the boy and rubbed her back. Skye stood there admiring them. "Listen up fellas!" yelled the coach as everyone gathered around. "We will be going to a tournament soon." Everyone cheered. "I know, I know you all must be excited but for the team, we will need to choose a captain." The field grew silent as everyone looked at each other. "There, there, don't be sad guys, I think we all know who is going to be captain," said Alex as he walked in pride towards the coach. "said who?" asked Ryle as he, too, walked towards the coach. "One of us will be captain this time," exclaimed Skye as he joined hands with Ryle. "It's good that you all are excited but the worthiest will get the position as team captain," the coach said in pride. "May the selections begin!" Everyone was thrilled with the announcement. The selection had a simple format. Their routine was usual but this time, the coach would grade them, their skills, their speed, and much more. As the routine started everyone was doing their best. "You good?" asked Ryle checking up on Aisha as she seemed exhausted. "Yeah, just need to catch my breath," Aisha reassured him as practice continued. Ryle cared for her more than he cared about anyone. After his mother's death, Ryle had made himself independent so that he could live without anyone, but now Aisha had become his necessity, just like water, food and oxygen; she had become a day-to-day need of his. Soon the class ended and for the first time, everyone dropped limp on the grass. "C'mon guys, it wasn't that exhausting," chuckled the coach. "I need someone to clean up after the cones placed in the fields any volunteers?" he asked. "Me and Ryle sir," said Aisha and tugged Ryle's arm. "Ugh okay," said Ryle as he stood up. "I'll join," smiled Skye. As everyone left the 3 kids stayed cleaning up the entire field. They cleaned it up and sat down on the grass. "You guys were awesome, I am so proud of you," said Aisha and looked at the boys. "You too miss aren't any less," chuckled Skye as Aisha turned red. "Who knows, maybe you'd become the captain," said Ryle as Skye nodded in agreement. "No, no I am not worthy to be to be captain. You guys were top-notch! I would like to have one of you as our captain," Aisha said with a smile on her face. "We will know tomorrow," said Skye as they all got up and headed home. Aisha wasn't feeling well; a flashback took over her. She sighed and sat on the bed. She felt torn. No matter how much time passed, no matter how many people she met she could never surpass that sickening feeling of loneliness. She couldn't get herself to forget about them. Can someone forget about their family? She took out her books and started studying so that it could distract her. But it was something else that took her mind off her dark thoughts. The girl was daydreaming about Skye. Another hopeless romantic. Being in love is messy. You never know who you're falling in love with but it's not a thing that we can control. Skye, in the meantime, was listening to music doing something he used to usually did. "Knock, knock," someone knocked on his door. Being given no reply, Eleonora walked in. "Skye! You need to reduce the volume of those damn headphones. You can barely hear anything!" "Sorry EI, but tell me why did you come in is there anything you need?" said the boy as he removed his headphones and sat up, straight. "Come down, we have a family dinner. You're the only one I want around as a family. Without you I won't go". She plastered a small smile on her face. Skye hugged her and ruffled her hair "How can I say no to you?" he chuckled. "Let's go". The kids walked down just to see their parents sitting around the dining table. The kids went and sat down. Skye looked around; everyone was eating peacefully as if nothing was wrong with them "we look like such a sweet and happy family," Mom said with a sweet smile. Skye looked at her with a bittersweet smile. "That's the issue. We look like a happy family, but we aren't. You guys are stupid money lovers that only care about their reputation and, of course, money, and who constantly neglect their two kids- a girl who tries to find love in everyone because no one ever loved her and a gay son. We might be filthy rich, but all this money is useless as hell," Skye wanted to get up and scream in their faces but this was sadly just in his thoughts. "Humanity is coming to a crash," said Skye's dad. "They elected a gay Mayor like can't people use their brains? "Why was he talking like gay was a slur" Skye looked at Eleonora for a bit of comfort. "IGNORE HIM" she mouthed. Eleonora knew about Skye, no, he hadn't told her, but it was obvious. She saw through him, she knew him because unlike her parents, she cared about him, and she wanted him to always be happy. "Fucking gays and their bullshit, it a mental illness I say mental ill-" Skye banged his arm's hard on the table and got up. The room was filled with silence, everyone looked at Skye who looked furious. "Excuse me, I need to go," Skye said as to went back to his room. "What's up with him?" Skye's mom asked. "Must have remembered his fight with Alex I will go check up on him," Eleonora covered up for him. She silently got up and followed her brother, "Are you okay?" Eleonora asked as she came inside the room and shut the door behind her. "What okay EI huh what!" Skye seemed frustrated as hell. "What's this man's problem I don't understand, not only is he unbothered about us but he also has to hate! He makes me so damn sick". "Calm down Skye ignore him, it doesn't matter," said EI as she sat on his bed. "It sickens me EI, why is society such a piece of shit," Skye said as he lay on his bed. "Society makes you stronger. It might seem horrible, but you know that it teaches you how harsh the world is and how strong you can be to deal with it," Eleonora smiled as she picked up Skye's head and placed it on her lap. "When did you grow up this much?" Skye felt proud. "Last time I checked, you were just a little girl crying because she hurt her finger," Skye chuckled. "Well, time changes everyone, doesn't it?" She caressed Skye's hair as he drifted to sleep. Aisha stayed awake dreaming about the one she loved. She was sitting on the balcony floor as the cold wind hit her face. Unwillingly, her body shivered. She was listening to soft music thinking about her prince charming, Skye. Her body melted in the soft embrace of the cold wind. Her eyes were shut as the wind blew her soft hair as they covered her face desperately to keep her face warm. She looked out from her balcony, seeing the flashing lights of the cars. She got up and went to bed. She lit a candle, switched off the lights, and fell asleep. Aisha loved him innocently; she had no bad intentions, but could you blame Skye for not feeling the same? As said, ultimately it wasn't in anyone's control. The day passed in a jiff, and everyone was hell of excited. Ryle, on the other hand, was nervous; he just didn't want anyone unworthy to become captain. The coach came around with a paper in his hand. "After I tell you who is the captain, he will put you in the positions that you will play in at the tournament, these may change at any time. So, without any further ado, I would like to announce that the team captain is…" Aisha squeezed her eyes shut as she held Ryle's hand tightly. "Ryle!" Ryle was left shocked "M-me? C- captain?" He stuttered. "Yes man!" Skye squealed and hugged Ryle. The kids cheered as Alex was enraged. Skye gave Alex a teasing look. "I am so proud of you won't I have a hug?" Said Aisha. "Of course!" Skye, Ryle, and Aisha hugged. Practice ended quickly as most of the time was spent on Ryle grading everyone to see in which place he would put them. Skye left a bit early, he said he wanted to go and get something. After a while, he returned with a bright red rose. Everyone's eyes were on him. He got on one knee holding the rose high "I can't hide it anymore, I love you I want to be with you, so on this fine day, I ask you, for the coming days will you be my date?" "Yes, yes a million times yes" Aisha squealed got down and hugged him with tears of happiness in her eyes.

Dating

Ryle's heart sank, all the happiness and excitement vanished in a second. Skye cupped Aisha's cheeks and kissed her in front of everyone. Alex was taken aback, wasn't Skye his boyfriend? Alex felt pissed, he grabbed his bag and left. Skye noticed and wanted to get up and stop him, but he couldn't. Not being able to analyze everything, he just stood there staring at them until Aisha came and hugged him. "I am so happy this is like the best day ever. You became captain and my Skye asked me out". My Skye… these words made Ryle bleed from inside. He mustered up the courage and gave Aisha a bittersweet smile "I am so happy for you guys," he broke their hug and looked at Aisha. "Are you happy?" she nodded, and Ryle smiled. Ryle went to Skye and patted his back "Congratulations to both of you," Ryle struggled to hold back his tears. "Congrats to you Captain," Skye said with a smile on his face. "I have got to go now," Ryle said as he bid his goodbyes and left. Ryle was broken, he felt horrible; he couldn't believe what had just happened. All his happiness of finally becoming captain had disappeared. He just wanted this day to end. The boy walked home while battling his tears. He got home and shut the door behind him. His drunkard father was not home. Ryle let out a sigh of relief. At least on this horrible day he wouldn't have to deal with his monster of a dad… He sat on his bed, took out a piece of paper and started to note down in which position he wanted to put everyone. Ryle wanted to throw Skye out of the team, but he knew it was wrong. No matter how much he tried to hate Skye, he couldn't. Skye was a good boy, kind to everyone Ryle held nothing against him. Ryle tried to take his mind from Aisha but the more he tried, the less it worked he just couldn't get her out of his mind. In the meantime, Skye was panicking. Alex did not reply to any of his messages, he just read them. "Did I mess up? Maybe I shouldn't have done it but all that I did, I did it for us". Skye was a mess; he knew Alex would be furious and scared of the consequences his actions might have. "Beep-beep" Skye's phone has a text message. Skye grabbed it hoping it was Alex and indeed it was. "Meet me at the field." Skye got up and grabbed his jacket, "El I am leaving it's urgent, cover up for me if anything happens". "What's up with him?" Eleonora wondered as she heard the door bang. Ryle was a mess; he couldn't handle it. For the first time, Ryle had given all his love to someone, and they had just given up on him. Ryle heard his father coming into the house and he was in no mood to deal with him. The boy got up, went to the bathroom, and locked the door. He felt weirdly safe there because his dad couldn't come in, there was no key, it was just locked from the inside. Ryle knew that because he used to hide there when he was a kid and his dad used to come home drinking. Ryle felt as if he was 10 again, hiding from his father's wrath. Ryle held the sink with both of his hands on each side and stared at himself. He didn't even recognize himself; his dark hair was a mess, his pale skin had turned crimson red from all the sobbing and his eyes were swollen. Though his muscular body looked the same he felt different. He felt like a whole other person. "What's wrong with me? Why can't anyone ever damn like me!" He punched the wall as blood trickled down his arm. "I just want to be damn loved. For once I like someone, I put all my love and all my care into her, and she chose him over me! Why can't I be better I am just the little messed-up boy that no one damn likes!" Ryle was a crying mess. He banged his back on the bathroom door and crouched down. The crying boy hugged his knees and cried. His hand was in tremendous pain and covered in blood, but he didn't care. He just rested his head on his knees while crying and didn't realize when he fell asleep. Emotional pain is always worse than physical pain. Feeling useless is a feeling no one should ever deal with. Ryle was an exception though. Poor boy didn't know why he was going through such a horrible time. He felt lonely alone, but don't you agree at the end of the day we are by ourselves? Skye ran to the field as fast as he could. He wanted to see Alex, hug him, kiss him, explain himself, and what not. As Skye reached, he saw Alex there waiting for him. "Alex!" He went and hugged Alex. "Get the hell away from me!" Alex pushed Skye away. "What in the goddamn world did you do today!? Are you in your right mind!? I can't even believe you." "Baby I can explain. It's not what you think-" "Don't baby me!" Alex cut him in. "For the past 1 year we have been damn perfect and suddenly this good-for-nothing girl comes, and you change!? I can't believe you Skye... We are over". "Wait baby, no listen." Tears rolled down Skye's eyes, so much so that he didn't realize it. "Stay away from me Skye" Alex muttered and started to walk away from Skye. "Alex, no, please listen to me for once-" Skye felt his left cheek burn. Alex had slapped him. "I said stay away," Alex said with a slightly raised voice and continued walking away. Skye cupped his left cheek as his knees grew numb and he fell down. "Alex please, I did it for us. So, we could be free. Alex please

Come back," Skye yelled but it was of no use Alex was gone... "I did it all for us," Skye mumbled as he lay sobbing under the stars alone this time. Skye meant no harm to anyone but now he knew he messed up big time. He had lost his whole damn world, his lover. As much as he wanted to, he couldn't hate Alex. He knew it was his fault and he had paid his price. Over an hour had passed and Eleonora was getting worried about Skye. Eleonora was at her room's balcony when she saw the silhouette of a man. His hair was a mess and he looked homeless. Eleonora squinted her eyes to see the man better and that's when she realized that man was none other than her brother. Eleonora rushed down the stairs making sure she didn't wake up her parents. She went downstairs and opened the door. Skye was a mess. Eleonora didn't ask or say anything, she just took his hand and got him to his room. She took him to the bathroom and washed his face. Skye stayed silent. They both went and sat on his bed. "Skye?" El caressed his hair "What's wrong?" "We broke up". Skye said with a numb face. "I am sorry to hear that. You know if you need anything I am here, right?" Eleonora said in hopes of comforting him. Skye looked at her as his eyes started to water. He hugged Eleonora and sobbed. El just rubbed his back, "Shhh, you're going to be okay, everything will be okay, trust me. Things always work out at the end, don't worry." Skye was already asleep. Eleonora held him in her arms until she was asleep too. Life fucks you up sometimes and it's nothing but a miserable piece of shit. "Ring ring," Skye's alarm rang. Skye didn't want to get up, he felt weak, but he knew he had no option as his parents wanted him to have a perfect attendance. He changed into some gray sweatpants and a green sweatshirt. At school, he noticed Aisha alone near the lockers. For the first time, she was alone; usually she used to be with Ryle. Skye felt like it was weird but walked up to Aisha. "Hey sweetheart," Aisha turned around saw Skye and hugged him. "Morning Skye," She broke the hug and looked at him. "You don't look that good. Are you okay?". "I am fine, don't worry about me," Skye looked away and then turned his gaze back at Aisha "There is something I got to ask you though." "What is it?" Aisha was filled with curiosity. "Can we take things slow between us…? It's just that my parents are pressurizing me and it's my-" Aisha pressed her index finger softly on Skye's lips. "Shh, no need to explain yourself, I understand," She smiled softly. Noticing their conversation from afar, Alex was fuming in jealousy and anger. There was no doubt that he still loved Skye endlessly, he was just pissed-off at him. It felt like Skye didn't value their relationship anymore. Even if Skye looked weak and tired in Alex's eyes, Skye still looked like a beautiful dream. So much love he had for Skye in his heart but whether he liked it or not he needed to let go.

The Trip

Weeks passed as Ryle dug his head into work as a captain. He grew distant from everyone. He barely talked to Aisha and sometimes talked to Skye. Meanwhile, Skye and Aisha grew closer to each other. Skye was desperately trying to forget about Alex because it seemed like Alex had already moved on. It was the day before the big trip. As the tournament was in a nearby city, they were going to go by bus, stay there for the night, play the next day, and return in the evening. The practice had ended as Ryle walked up in front of everyone to give a short speech. "I am not here to bore you guys out. As you all may know by now, tomorrow we are going to the tournament. I want no misbehavior on the bus or when we reach. I am not looking for fights. No matter what happens, we will stick together as a team. I want you guys to go out there and do your best. I don't care if we win or not, I just want us to go out there and rock. We got this!" With that, he ended his speech and walked away to the coach's office. Aisha's eyes were glistening. She felt motivated by Ryle. He indeed made a good captain. Aisha and Skye started to walk home together. "I am so proud of Ryle. It's his first time as captain and he is doing so damn good," Skye exclaimed. "I know right? I can't wait for him to act as captain tomorrow." That's when Aisha realized that she had forgotten her bag back at the field. "Skye, I forgot my bag back at the field. You go home and I will go get it okay?" Skye just nodded as Aisha ran back to the field. Aisha searched around for her bag and after a lot of trying she finally found it. "There you are," she saw her bag, picked it up, and smiled. With the corner of her eye, she noticed Ryle doing something in a corner. She silently walked up to him and peeked in front; Ryle was smoking. "Ryle! Don't do that," she slapped the cigarette out of his hand. "Do you know how much they can harm you!? You must run tomorrow, why are you damaging your lungs for no reason? I am worried about you. What's wrong? You have been acting distant for days now. If anything is going on, you can tell me, talk to me." Ryle looked at her with dead eyes. "Why do you care?"

Aisha's heart got heavy. "There is no need to act like you care I can take care of myself". Ryle coldly walked away. Aisha was taken aback by his words. Unwantingly, she teared up. It reminded her of how she had fought with her friends. Aisha didn't know how to react. With tears in her eyes, she took her bag and headed home. Ryle was fuming. He tried to calm himself down on the way back home, but it all got ruined when he saw his father lying drunk on the couch as usual. It irritated him. He knew that deep down it was all his father's fault for what he was going through. He went into his room, banging the door. He threw his bag down and rubbed his temples in desperation to calm himself down. He couldn't get Aisha's words out of his mind. His temper increased to the point that he couldn't control himself anymore. "You don't! You don't! You don't! You don't get to act like you care," he punched the wall until his hand was covered in blood. He numbly started at his now bleeding hand. "You don't get to act like you care and then forget me as soon

The Trip

as someone came." He looked down at his aching knuckles. Ryle wanted to cry and scream but he just couldn't let his tears fall. He washed the blood and bandaged his hand. He ate some canned beans and sat on his bed thinking about the coming day. He didn't care about studying when he had such an important tournament coming up. He was excited for the trip but that's when Aisha came into his mind again. He didn't blame her for liking Skye; the issue was that he felt left out. He didn't want to be alone (Ryle was sensitive). He lay on his bed still thinking about Aisha and slowly slipped into an angelic sleep. Aisha, in the meantime, was overthinking everything. Her old friends kept coming back to her mind. She couldn't understand what was wrong with Ryle. She just kept blaming herself like the last time with her friends. She looked over at the clock and it was midnight. Tomorrow she would have a long day, so she closed her eyes while thinking about her Ryle. Blaming yourself is wrong, things don't change if you blame on yourself. I think this is something we all know but why do we still do it? The big day was finally here. In the morning around 05.00 am everyone was at school. Aisha was with Skye but kept looking over at Ryle to see if she could get a chance to talk with him, but Ryle was busy checking if everyone was there or not. The bus was finally here. "Guys, one by one get in the bus and as soon as you all take a seat, I will count you all," said Ryle as everyone walked in the bus. After counting everyone, their journey started. The team's sweethearts sat together holding hands and surprisingly Ryle was forced to sit with Alex. They played songs, sang, and even danced inside the bus. They were having a whole damn party over there. Weirdly Ryle and Alex started to get along and Skye for sure didn't like it, though he was happy for Alex deep inside. Aisha was lost in

Skye's eyes. She was blinded by love so much that Ryle was sure she had forgotten completely about him. "C'mon captain, dance with us," squealed Alex. "Let me show you," Ryle chuckled, got up, and started dancing as the entire bus was cheering for him. They were having a blast, but soon they reached. "Everyone get down, one by one. You can roam around if you want but be here in front of the bus in 15 minutes." Everyone got down but that's when Skye realized that he had forgotten his hat. "Aisha, I forgot my hat, I might have dropped it." "Go get it. I will roam around a bit and see you in 15 minutes, okay?" Skye nodded and went towards the bus. When he got there, he couldn't find it, so he decided to look around. Out of nowhere, someone grabbed his arm and kissed him. Skye knew those lips better than anyone. Alex pulled Skye closer, kissing his lips harsher than before. His hands traveled around Skye's body feeling the intimacy that they hadn't felt in weeks. Alex grabbed Skye's sunshine-bright hair and pulled it harshly. "I missed you so much baby boy. For how long I can stay mad on this face" Alex touched Skye's chin and lifted it before smashing his lips again on Skye's as they both fell together in the last seat. Skye had ached for Alex's touch for weeks. "Alex, enough," Skye broke their kiss. "They will be waiting for us we need to go," Alex nodded as they both got up. "Don't do shit again," Alex said and pecked Skye's lips before getting off the bus. Skye fixed his clothes still having butterflies and got off the bus as soon as he couldn't see Alex. They went and joined the others as the coach walked up in front of everyone. "I will separate you into different dorms and by 10.00 PM I want you all to go and sleep. Let's all be fresh for tomorrow," the coach said and segregated them all in their dorms. Aisha, Ryle, Skye and even Alex were put in different dorms. "12.00 am in front of the washroom," Alex whispered in a low tone and went to his dorm. Soon the time came and the two forbidden lovers held each other in a sweet embrace. "I missed you Alex," Skye mumbled. "Me more, baby boy, me more," Alex smiled. They were around a forest, so they decided to go there and be safe from everyone's gaze. Skye held Alexs's hand and led him inside the dark forest. They lay on the grass cuddling each other unbothered about the creepy darkness around them. Suddenly breathing sounds were heard and they felt someone's gaze on them. "What was that?" Skye looked terrified towards Alex.

The Tournament

*I*t was late at night around midnight when Ryle heard someone outside. He didn't want his team to get in trouble. The dark-haired boy swiftly got up and went outside. He saw 2 silhouettes in the darkness going into the forest. "What are you doing here?" He heard Aisha's angelic voice. He adored her voice; her voice was sweet but not childish. Infact, he admired not just her voice, but everything about her.- Her smile, her silky dark brown hair, her short height, even her black eyes that seemed like an endless whirlpool of darkness. He turned around, looking at her with ice-cold eyes, whether he wanted it or not he had to hold himself to back up. Was it for him? Was it for Skye? Or even Aisha? He didn't know, the only thing that was understandable was that it was the correct or rather appropriate thing to do. "Go sleep it's late you don't want to get in trouble," he muttered in an ice-cold voice. "You are out too, and I certainly don't want to go tell on you, so let me stay," Aisha gave him a playful smile as Ryle rolled his eyes. "Just stay silent and don't create any damn issue. Remember don't you dare disobey me," Ryle said in a deep husky voice as Aisha got shivers down her spine and nodded. They both went into the forest with Ryle in the lead. Ryle walked forward and saw Skye lying on Alex as if they were fighting. "Guys, enough you can't be fighting in the middle of the night," Ryle lunged at Skye and pulled him away from Alex as Alex got into the act of getting hit by Skye. "Get off me, blondie," Alex's voice was filled with hatred. Skye felt torn apart from his lover, he just wanted to hold him in his embrace but couldn't. Alex glared at him to start the act. Aisha ran over to Skye. "Are you okay?" In a panicked voice, she scanned Skye's face for any wounds. Ryle checked up on Alex to see if he was okay. Skye looked at Aisha, "I am okay don't worry." As they all got up, Ryle said, "I won't talk about this anymore. All three of you go to your dorms and if I see you out again you will be kicked out of the team". Silence filled up the night. "Ryle…" Aisha exclaimed in a terrified tone "From where did we come?" Ryle looked around and that's when he realized that they were lost. "Let's just stay together because if they find us, we'll be dead," Alex said and everyone got serious. The teenagers started to walk around, trying to find a way out of that dark maze. A sound was heard as Ryle stepped in front to protect everyone. "Get behind me," he exclaimed. Everyone was scared. "It's late at midnight and there might be dangerous animals in the forest Let's just stay put," Aisha said and put her hand on Ryle's shoulder pulling him back. "We can't," Ryle said in that same cold tone. "Why, though? It seems like a good idea," Skye said, trying not to lose hope. "If they find us here, we will all be eliminated from the tournament," Ryle sighed frustrated. The night grew silent again. From the corner of his eye, Alex noticed a small light "Hey bozoz, I see a small light". "Alex don't go alone," Ryle tried to explain but it was no use; Alex had already started to follow the light and forcefully everyone else followed. Luckily it was the dorm's light and all of them were finally back to safety. "You guys need not thank me, I know we are all saved because of me and gladly you are all welcomed," Alex said once again, taking pride in himself. "We would not have been lost in the first place if it wasn't for you," Aisha was quick to reply. "Oh did you forget your Loverboy?" Aisha rolled her eyes. Skye loved being called Loverboy not for Aisha, but for Alex, his actual love. "Enough you both! Dorms now and if I see you out before sunrise you all are out!" Ryle threatened as they all headed to their dorms. Skye was awake, lost in his thoughts. He was grateful to have gotten together with Alex again. Oh how much he had missed him, missed his touch, his soft words, everything about him. He had ached to be with him again and finally, he got what he had longed for. Sunshine caressed Aisha's soft skin as she woke up. She sat on her bed, looking around and surprisingly no one was there. It quickly hit her that everyone was out practicing. She tied her hair into a slick ponytail, and wore a top and leggings before going and joining the others. "You are late," Ryle glared at her "Sorry captain, I overslept," Aisha looked down, feeling a bit guilty. Ryle's eyes softened at the state of her. "Join the others," he ordered as practice continued. This tournament was important to Ryle as this would show his ability as a captain and the boy just wanted to feel like a worthy person. Time came around as all the teams were now on the field, waiting to be paired. As soon as Ryle's team was paired and soon, they were on the field, waiting for their match to start. "Guys you got this. No matter how this match turns out remember we are a team. Aisha on defense, Alex good luck goalkeeping, we believe in you and Skye stay with me and back me up". "Got it captain," Skye nodded as the match started. The match started smoothly but soon took a turn for the worse. The score, from 3-0, soon turned into 3-3. It was a tie and that was sadly not enough. Though Ryle's team was doing okay, Sid, one of their strongest players, was injured and the team had lost a lot of motivation. "Time out!" Ryle yelled out as everyone fell tired to the ground. "Guys I want to speak to you." Hearing their captain, everyone sat up straight. "We need this win for the finals," he roared. "I have spent weeks training you for this. I know Sid is injured but we need to keep our morale up. We have little time left. Don't fail me." Everyone went back to the field. The match continued and there was just 1 minute left. Skye had the ball as he dribbled across the entire field by himself. The goalkeeper was impressed by the boys' skills and felt proud. Skye passed the ball to Ryle in a last hope of winning. Ryle got the ball, swung his leg back, and with all his force kicked the ball. "GOALLL !" Alex yelled and a smile plastered on his face. He ran and hugged Ryle as Aisha went and congratulated Skye. They had made it to the finals. Ryle was shocked; it was the first time Alex had shown any affection towards the team. Ryle hugged him back as their team celebrated. Everyone sat and relaxed under the shade of a big tree. "Good work captain," Aisha patted Ryle's back. Ryle gave her a sweet simile. "It was all because of you guys, and I am so proud of you all. I am proud of you all." The team rested for a while but was soon called on. Ryle was ready to face the new team, but little did he know that this team was not easy to take down. Before the match started, Ryle gathered the team once again to motivate them. "Here he goes with the pep talk," Alex rolled his eyes. Alex wasn't the type of guy who needed motivation, he needed to be pushed to do something. He didn't believe in words, he considered it a waste of time. "Alex, you said something?" Ryle glared at Alex. "N-no sir" Alex was taken aback, his captain's eyes viciously piercing through him. "Better," Ryle muttered. "After all the training finally, the finals are here. To be honest, I don't care if we win or lose. All I want from you guys is to do your best, and try your best. At the end of the day, that is all that matters. We are a team for a reason, I depend on you guys. Don't fail me." Ryle's words had a weird sense to them. They were motivational but also filled with hope, support, and pride. Alex always wanted to be captain, so when Ryle was announced captain, he wasn't quite happy about it, but whether he liked it or not, Ryle indeed was a great leader.

Everyone took their places. The opponent team seemed vicious "They certainly won't be easy to defeat," Ryle murmured under his breath as the match started. The opponent team was skilled, they didn't lose 1 goal, but Alex wasn't weaker. The score was 0-0 and no matter how hard each team tried, their trial was in vain. "What's wrong with these assholes? Why aren't they letting us win?" a boy from the opponent team exclaimed. Hearing that, Aisha fumed with anger. How dare they say something like that! Aisha was a defender, but she didn't care. She ran ahead with all her might, snatching the ball from the boys' legs and dribbling it alone across the entire team. Not only was Ryle in shock, but all the others too. They just stood there staining. The girl dribbled the ball and stood near the goalpost. "This is for you guys!" she yelled and swung her leg back, kicking the ball with all her force. The ball went in and everyone was left staring. Without missing a beat, Alex ran to Aisha and picked her up on his shoulders. "What you looking at? We won!" He cheered as the entire team circled them and started cheering. Ryle couldn't believe it; his hard work had finally paid off. Watching his team, he never felt prouder. Aisha looked at Alex who was holding her and had a huge smile on her face. She felt at the top of the world. Aisha looked around and saw the opponent team mad. She looked at the captain. He seemed familiar. On looking closer it hit her, he was Jasmine's big brother! She looked around in hopes of seeing her friend. There they were, all three of them together. Aisha didn't believe her eyes, she rubbed them thinking it was a dream, but it wasn't. She quickly got down from Alex's shoulders and rushed towards them. "Jasmine, Lily, Rose!?" She said as she back hugged Jasmine. "I missed you guys so much!" Aisha teared up. Jasmine held Aisha's hand and slowly turned around.

Reunion

Jasmine's hands were cold, the soft warmth that used to be in her hands wasn't there anymore. "Aisha…" Jasmine looked towards her. There was no sign of emotion on her face. She looked numb. Lily and Rose stayed quiet. Aisha quickly wiped her tears and smiled, "I missed you guys so much. How are you? Did you miss me? How's the pipe? Oh, I can't wait to catch up with you gu…" "No," Jasmine muttered coldly. Aisha's heart started racing; she didn't know what to say. "You left us," Jasmine said, her voice filled with hatred. "Didn't you care about us?" I see you have found new people here. Good for you don't come to us though. We don't care anymore. "Jas, no, I never wanted to leave you guys. I want us, I want us back," Aisha was yet again cut off. "Us? We are not friends anymore. We were, now we are nothing but strangers." Rose was harsh and cold. Her words pierced Aisha's heart like a poisoned blade that would slowly kill her. Aisha looked at Lily in hopes of getting support, but Lily just looked down. "Guys please, I missed you all too much to let you go, not again please," Aisha pleaded but it was of no use. "Aisha, I think you should go…" Lily looked away with tears in her eyes. Aisha was taken aback. She didn't expect them to react this way; she regretted having gone up to them. She looked at the team who were still celebrating, a small smile crept up on her face but the pain she was feeling was getting worse. Aisha ran, she just wanted to be as far as possible from there. Ryle saw Aisha going away but couldn't understand why. He followed her into the woods but suddenly lost sight of her. "Where the hell is she gone now?" Ryle muttered under his breath. On moving forward, he noticed a small silhouette of a girl crouched down and crying. "Aisha…..?

Skye and Alex were still busy celebrating their win, the team was on top of the world. While celebrating though Skye bumped into someone: "Watch where you're going mate!" the guy roared. "Sorry," Skye mumbled, a bit intimidated. "Sorry!? You think I will let you go away that easily?" The boy started walking intimidatingly towards Skye. Alex noticed Skye getting uncomfortable and walked over to him. "Break it up you two, I apologize from his side. Let us all just go back to our teams." The guy looked like the goalkeeper of the opponent's team. He looked strong and well-built, that's why Alex was in no mood to get into a fight. Alex could easily win in a fight with this guy, but he didn't want it to ruin the day for his team. "I forgive you, no big deal, you are lucky we let you win this time, or else with this blonde, you guys are just sore losers," the guy flicked Skye's head hurt causing Skye to yell with pain. Alex was enraged by his words and the boy's actions just made it worse. "No one touches my boy," Alex spat out and gritted his teeth before lunging onto the goalkeeper.

Aisha looked at Ryle, her eyes were red from all the tears that escaped her eyes. Ryle's heart was torn apart seeing the girl he loved the most in tears. She wasn't his but that didn't mean that he didn't care. Whether his or not, he would always love her, she would always be his love, his admiration, his inspiration, his savior, and even his life. "What's wrong?" Ryle asked, softening his voice as he sat near the girl. Her hair was messy, her nose was red, and even her eyes were puffy but still, that didn't stop her beauty from shining from within. "My friends, th-they-" she couldn't continue as she burst sobbing. Ryle gently took her in his embrace, "Shh, calm down then we will talk, okay?" he rubbed Her back, hoping that would calm her down. A while passed as they both held each other. Aisha caught her breath and spoke, "I met my old friends. but... but they-" she sobbed. "Until and unless you don't calm down, we can't talk. Catch your breath. Come on, now, take deep breaths with me," Ryle and Aisha both took deep breaths together as Aisha slowly calmed down and was ready to talk. "I met my friends," she mumbled in soft voice. I tried talking to them, but they didn't want to talk. It's just that I didn't expect them to reject me like that... I thought we would be the same but... but they just pushed me away like we were nothing," Aisha sobbed on Ryle's chest. Ryle rubbed her back. "Things change Aisha, you can't expect everything to be the same way you left them. I know it's hard but when something disappoints you, but you can do nothing about it, the best thing to do is to divert yourself. No matter how much we try, we can't turn back time, we need to come in terms with reality," Aisha softly shed tears on Ryle's chest. She knew that what he was saying was correct, but she didn't care, she just needed someone to hold and sob her eyes out.

Alex lunged at the other goalkeeper "How dare you lay hands on him huh!? Who do you think you are!? I have been keeping my cool, but you pushed me to my limits." Alex kept punching the boy and it soon turned into a fistfight. Alex couldn't control his anger when it came to Skye; the only person who could lay a finger on him was Alex and when it was someone else, Alex would lose it. Skye just stood there staring at the two boys fighting. He did not know what to do, he just froze in his place. Soon people gathered around, and some even tried to separate them, but it was no use. The only person that could separate them was Ryle. A boy went in search of Ryle. Meanwhile, Ryle had calmed down Aisha and was ready to head back. "Ryle!" the boy yelled out. "What's wrong? Is everything okay?" Ryle patted the boy's back. "Alex got into a fight and there is no one who can pull them apart. Please come, " the boy managed to say while panting. Ryle froze, he couldn't believe that even after winning, Alex had managed to get into a fight. Enraged, Ryle ran back to camp just to see Alex beating the other team's goalkeeper mercilessly. "Alex, enough. Get off him," Ryle held Alex's shoulder and pulled him back. The other boy quickly got up, wiping his bleeding nose. "You guys are beasts! Look what he has done to me!" the bruised boy said. "And I can do even more so SQUIRM" Alex yelled in a terrifying tone as the other boy ran. Ryle looked at Alex, enraged, and gave him a tight slap across his right cheek. "Are in you your right mind Alex! Fighting with strangers? You could have gotten seriously hurt," Ryle roared. Alex just looked down silently. He knew that he was at fault and that he could have controlled himself. Alex felt a bit guilty as he could have gotten the whole team in trouble. "The boy started to fight with me first, Alex Just stood up for me," Skye reasoned. "I understand but that was no way to react," Ryle said in a stern tone. "Sorry," Alex spat out. "It's fine," Ryle sighed "Skye, find Aisha and go pack your bags. We need to head home in an hour. Pack mine and Alex's bags too if you can. I am going to take Alex to the infirmary. Make sure everyone is on the bus in an hour". "Yes captain," Skye replied as he headed towards the dorms. Ryle held Alex's bicep and took him to the infirmary. Ryle was worried that Alex was injured. They went to the infirmary and the doctor started treating Alex's wounds. "Alex, you need to take better care of yourself. I understand you got mad, but you could get in some serious trouble," Ryle sat down on a chair. "I apologize, captain, my intentions weren't wrong. I just wanted to protect Skye," Alex muttered in a guilty voice. "It's okay, just control yourself next time" Ryle pat Alex's shoulder. After a while, everyone was gathered on the bus as Alex and Ryle joined them. After the headcount, they started to head home. Aisha cuddled next to Skye as he caressed her soft brown hair. Aisha softly drifted to sleep. She had had a hard day, and being in the arms of the boy she loved the most felt like heaven. Ryle looked at them, eyes filled with love. He wanted to be Skye but as long as he could just feel Aisha's presence, it was enough for him. Sometimes we love someone without knowing whether they will love us back. I think that's true love, loving someone and wanting them to be happy, whether it is with or without you. It was late at night when they all reached. Everyone took their bags and headed home. Skye and Ryle were to check if someone had forgotten something. "All's set! Everyone took their belongings," Skye said with a grateful smile. Ryle looked at Skye and nervously pressed his lips together, "I know." Skye looked at him confused, "What Ryle?" Ryle looked at him and sighed, "I am not an idiot Skye; I know about you and Alex."

Abusive

Skye froze. He felt like someone had torn open his chest. Ryle would now expose them and all their fights, all their struggles would be of no use now. "R-Ryle I can explain," that was the only thing Skye managed to say before silence filled up the night. Skye looked down picking on his skin as Ryle stared at him with mixed emotions. Ryle was confused, curious and disappointed in Skye for hiding it and going behind Aisha's back." "Ryle, I know that you might not support it but it's something I have to do," Skye tried justifying his actions. "My parents don't support me. If they found out, I don't know what would happen." "Does Aisha know?" Ryle asked. Skye shook his head. Ryle ran his fingers through his hair to calm himself down. He looked at Skye, his eyes were filled with rage, worry, and pity. "Skye, do you realize what you are doing is wrong? She loves you more than herself and you are using her emotions for your benefit? I can't believe you." Ryle looked away in frustration. "I have no other option, Ryle, and you know it. You know how my father is, he wants me to be perfect and I can't. Using Aisha is the only way I can be with Alex. Please try to understand, I don't mean to harm anyone, and you know it," Skye sighed. "If you want to go and tell her, go. You know now, you, can go tell anyone you want". Ryle looked at him in disbelief. "I am not that type of person who goes and tells about you. I am your friend, and I will support you no matter what. Just don't hurt her, I can't bear to watch her suffer anymore." Skye smiled, "Thank you Ryle, it means a lot to me."

Time passed as both boys went home. Ryle lay on his bed as many thoughts were running through his head. He wanted to go and reveal everything to Aisha, but he knew he couldn't. He had given Skye his word.

Aisha stayed staring at the ceiling. She had a tiring day. Although she enjoyed it, she could not get the encounter with her friends out of her mind. Alisha clenched her eyes shut, trying to forget everything that had happened. Sometimes it's not good living in the past. It doesn't let you enjoy the present. No matter how much we think about our past, there is nothing we can do to change it. Eyes shut tight, the girl softly fell asleep. The next day rolled around as the team gathered after school. Everyone was still busy congratulating each other as the coach told everyone to gather around. "Our win yesterday was massive. I cannot tell you how proud I am. A round of applause for your captain who trained you, supported you, and cheered for you." The team clapped as Skye whistled. "Your trophy will be placed beside all the other team's achievements. I hope we keep moving forward like this." Without wasting any time, the training began. "Aisha you good?" Ryle asked. He just wanted to check up on her, and make sure she was okay. Aisha nodded with a smile. Soon, the practice ended. Skye said he had some work to do and stayed late while Ryle and Aisha walked together. "Thank you for yesterday, Ryle, I don't know what I would do without you," Aisha gave him a soft smile. "Don't thank me, I just want you to know that, through your lows and highs I will always be by your side. If you ever need anything I am here. Trust me, you would have done the same". Aisha would have done the same but that wasn't the reason Ryle was doing it. The reason was much deeper, much more sensitive, and much more heart-warming. Aisha hugged Ryle "You are the best Ryller," Ryle held her tight in his arms as her hair smelled like flowers. Aisha's head was on Ryle's chest as Ryle caressed her hair. He wanted to scream and tell her 'I LOVE YOU' but he knew that he just couldn't and that was eating him up from Inside.

Skye sneaked out of the football field and went near a hill. The hill was deserted, that's why. Skye had planned to meet Alex there. Skye was scared. How would he tell Alex that their secret was out? Skye knew that Ryle wouldn't reveal their secret, but Alex didn't trust anyone. Alex was aggressive; there was a reason he was a bully so Skye already knew that this wouldn't end well. "Skye," Alex said with a bright smile, picking up the blonde lad in his arms. Skye and Alex hugged each other as Alex sat down embracing the blonde boy in his arms "I am so proud of you, you rocked yesterday!" Alex praised. "If it wasn't for your mighty arms, we would have lost," Skye giggled. "By the way are your wounds better now? that guy seemed tough yesterday?" Alex gave a warm smile to Skye, "I am okay don't worry remember the only person that can lay hands on you is me." That sent shivers down Skye's spine; he gulped "I g…got to tell you Sss…something," Skye stuttered. "What's up?" Alex sat up straight with a serious look on his face. Brows furrowed, he poked the inside of his check with his tongue. "Ryle knows," Skye spat out. Alex got up with a jerk, making Skye fall to the ground. Alex grabbed Skye from the collar. "Ryle knows what?" Alex gritted his teeth. "I am s-sorry I d- didn't tell him. He found out I swear!" the blonde boy's bottom lip trembled. Alex was enraged. Their secret was all out because of a tiny mistake. In his eyes, it was Skye's fault that Ryle knew. Alex saw nothing but fires of rage. He raised his hand high and slapped the back of Skye's head. Skye's head hung low, knowing there was nothing he could do about the enraged beast in front of him. Alex's hand grew into a fist as it rained down the blonde lad's face. Alex had lost control of his temper. He kept hitting Skye's arms, back, and legs without thinking that it was his lover whom he was harming. Alex kept beating Skye as the blonde had no energy to react. Alex let go of Skye's collar and the boy fell limp on the ground. His nose was bleeding, body was covered with bruises the blonde shot his eyes tightly in desperation to endure the tremendous pain his body was going through. Alex stared at his bleeding lover from him with no mercy in his eyes. It wasn't that Alex hated him, Alex loved him more than he could love anyone; it was just that his anger had taken over him, and when Alex was angry there was nothing worse than him. Alex lay near the bleeding boy as Skye was too scared to even open his eyes. Alex soon came to his senses after seeing Skye bleed. Alex's anger was replaced with worry as he shook Skye's numb body. "Please, no more," the blonde mumbled weakly under his breath. Alex barely heard the lad's faint words; he picked up Skye in his arms, making sure that he wasn't hurting him more. Alex's house wasn't away from the hill, so he took Skye there. Alex's parents were out of town so there would be no one to disturb them. Alex carried the boy to his bedroom and softly placed him on the bed. "I am going out to buy you some medicine," Alex said while taking out some money from his wallet. He held Skye's chin tightly and made the blonde face him. "Don't you dare move from here or it won't end well," Alex bit the inside of his cheek and let go of Skye's chin. Skye dug his face into the soft pillow on Alex's bed. Alex went to the pharmacy and bought everything that he would need to heal Skye's wounds. Moon high, it was night now. The city lit up with all types of lights. Alex walked down the road as he came across a pastry shop. Alex sighed and went inside. He remembered how much Skye loved cakes and decided to buy him a small pastry. As Alex went home, he noticed that Skye was still on the bed and had not moved a bit, the poor boy was still trembling terrified of Alex. Alex's eyes softened at Skye's state. "Baby?" He said in a sweet voice. Skye softly got up and sat straight. Alex sat on the bed, "Remove your shirt." Skye struggled in lifting his arms. Watching his boy struggle, Alex quickly rushed in and helped him remove his shirt. Skye grunted in pain. "There …there it's okay now," Alex comforted him as he placed the blonde's shirt on the nightstand. Alex opened the bag he had bought from the pharmacy and took out some antiseptic with cotton. Skye whimpered in fear, knowing that the antiseptic would hurt. Alex poured the antiseptic on the cotton. "Get ready this will hurt". Alex pressed the soaked cotton on Skye's paper-like skin. Skye hissed in pain. "It hurts Alex, it hurts so bad," Skye whimpered as the cotton burnt his skin. "I am almost done, love. See I told you; you shouldn't have made me mad." Alex continued cleaning his wounds. "It's okay, it will burn now but soon the sting will be gone. Skye stayed silent, biting his bottom lip. Alex cleaned Skye's wounds and soon started bandaging them. Alex heard Skye sniffling as he looked up to see warm tears rushing down the blonde's face. Alex cupped his cheek with one hand and wiped her tears. "I am almost done," Alex put the antiseptic with the bandages near the bed and took out the pastry. "You are in a lot of pain today so take some rest and have this," he handed Skye the pastry. Skye's face brightened as he took the pastry from Alex. "Thank you so much!". Alex smiled seeing the boy happy as he sat near him pulling him on his lap. "Eat up, it's late, stay here for the night," Alex caressed the blonde lad's back; Skye nodded. Soon, their night was coming to an end as both held each other through the cold and lonely night.

Eleonora was worried, sobbing in her room thinking the worst about her brother. Her parents were making random calls searching for their son but there was no sign of him. Eleonora did not want to see anyone. She locked herself in her room, crying to comfort herself. The girl cried herself to sleep that night. Maybe after the clock hits 12, the world changes, or at least new hopes arise. Hopes that this cruel world will turn sweet or better someday. "Where is this boy?" Skye's father grunted in anger. "Wait till he comes back home. I will see to where he spent his night!" He banged his hand on the table.

Soon Exams

The night passed quickly. Skye opened his eyes and found himself in Alex's arms. Alex was already awake caressing, his lover's hair. "Morning Sunshine," Alex whispered in Skye's ear. "Why are you up so early?" Skye whimpered, adjusting himself in Alex's arms. "To take care of you. I didn't want to be asleep when you woke up," Alex pecked Skye's eyes. "Are your wounds better?" Skye nodded. Alex lifted Skye off his lap and removed Skye's bandages to check up on his wounds. "They look much better but keep them bandaged for at least another week." Alex started to clean Skye's wounds again. Skye groaned in discomfort and started to move around. "Don't move!" Alex said sternly as he bandaged the blonde's wounds. "You are all good," Alex smiled as Skye scooted closer to him, putting his head on Alex's chest. "Want to bunk school with me today?" Alex asked, caressing the blond lad's back. "I can't, Alex. My parents want me to have full attendance." It suddenly hit Skye, "Oh shit, they must be freaking out I didn't go home last night." Panicked, he got up from the bed looking for his bag. "Alex, I can't find my bag. My father is going to kill me for not going home yesterday" Skye was panicking as Alex came near him and hugged him. "Take my bag it's okay, yours must be at home don't worry." Alex gripped Skye's jaw tightly "And if that bastard father of yours lays a finger on you, I will tear his arms out." Skye smiled and kissed him "Thank you". The blond wore an oversized sweatshirt and soon left his lover's house.

Aisha smiled as she crouched down and plucked a flower. "Pretty," she mumbled. For some reason, she felt happy. "What's with all the smiles today?" Ryle asked admiring her. "I don't know Ryle, I just feel so happy today". Aisha looked at him holding the flower in her hand. Ryle took the flower from her soft hands and put it behind her ear. "Whether a reason of your happiness or not, I am just glad to see you happy." Skye saw them and went up to them. "Anyone missed me?" he smiled as Aisha hugged him. "Of course, I did." She noticed the bandages on his arms. "Who did that to you? Are you okay?" she asked, worried. "I fell from my cycle, don't worry your Skye is strong," he replied with a confident smile. Skye was a good liar; he had the best excuses to get himself out of things. I guess that's what happens when you have 2 pathological liars for parents. Aisha cupped Skye's right cheek. "Take care okay, I don't want to see you in pain." Ryle felt like a third wheel and unwillingly backed off. Soon the bell rang and all three of them went to their classes. It was lunch and the trio met up to talk with each other. They sat around a table to eat. Ryle was lost in his world. "Hey Ryle, what's wrong? You seem tensed," Skye asked worriedly. "I am not okay! Did you hear? Our exams are starting in two weeks". Aisha spat out her food to "What?" Skye chucked and wiped her mouth "You guys are going to be just fine okay," Skye smiled. "Skye, brother, you are a top scorer we are not!" Ryle said putting his hand on Skye's back. "Ryle do you want us to study together, after school in general", Aisha asked Ryle. Ryle felt flustered by the question. "Of course," he said with a smile. "I can't, my parents won't let me," Skye lied. His parents couldn't care less but he didn't want to make Alex angry. "It's okay, Skye, we understand," Aisha kissed his cheek. "Hence plans are made. After school I will meet Ryle and we will discuss when to study together." Ryle nodded. Soon school ended but there was no football class. The trio scattered into 2. Skye went home as Ryle and Aisha went on a walk together.

Skye was scared to go home. He knew his dad would certainly not react pleasantly. He stood in front of his front door, hands trembling. There was nothing he could do now, sooner or later he would have to face his father's wrath. The lad took a deep breath and walked into his house. At first, he saw no one but as his eyes moved around, he saw his dad's silhouette sitting on the dining table. The boy locked eyes with his father. His dad seemed furious as if someone had stolen the most precious thing from him and he was out for revenge. "Look who decided to come!" Skye's father roared as he banged his hand on the table. The blonde flinched to the sound. His father walked towards him as if each step was giving a life-threatening threat. "Where were you last night huh?" his dad yelled. The boy's bottom lip quivered. He noticed his mother come out of a room. She had a look of disappointment on her face. Skye didn't understand why, what was his fault in wanting to be away from his neglecting family? If maybe she had loved him even a bit, this wouldn't have happened. "Answer me!" his father yelled, bringing his mind back on track. He looked up to see his father's fuming eyes that looked at him with hatred. How could he look at his own son with this much hatred? His own damn son! "Skye!" He heard a voice coming from the staircase. He saw a worried Eleonora run down the stairs. Eleonora ran up to him and hugged him. "Where were you? How are you? What are these bandages? Are you hurt?" she bombarded him with questions. A smile crept up on Skye's lips "I am fine, yesterday I fell and hurt myself while coming back. That's why I spent the night in a hospital." Skye glared at his father "You should rest right now," El took him to his room, sitting near him.

Ryle and Aisha walked together in an empty street. The sun was setting and the moon could be seen faintly. The cold wind made the leaves rustle. Surprisingly, there were no cars on the road. It was like time had stopped just for them, so the world could be all theirs. Aisha took a deep breath. as the cold air filled up her lungs. Her hair brushed against her blood-red cheeks. "This day is pretty, isn't it?" she said looking around the dead road. "Not as pretty as the world I see in your eyes," Ryle wanted to say he struggled to hold himself back. "It is," he smiled looking at her. He wasn't even looking around. His eyes were fixated on his world. "It's my first time giving exams. I didn't think we had them," Aisha whined. They both found a bench to sit on and rested there. "So, how are we going to plan this," Ryle ran his hand through his hair. "Every day after school we meet up at my place and study," Aisha shrugged her shoulders. "And suffer you mean," Ryle sighed dramatically. "Oh, come on, it can't be that bad!" Aisha patted his back "I will help you through it, don't worry Ryle." Ryle looked into her sweet, honey-like eyes. "Thanks, Aisha, you have helped me a lot you know". Aisha's lips curled into a smile. "You support me at my lowest. You are the moon in my darkest nights this is the least I can do for you". They just stared into each other's eyes for a moment. Ryle held his urge to kiss the brunette's cherry lips. He was like a tied-up horse, wanting to be set free. Suddenly Aisha heard meowing noises. "Do you hear it? What's that?" Aisha got up and looked around. Ryle was confused as he sat there. Aisha looked around and behind a bush, she found a small kitten. Aisha took it in her arms. "Look what I found," she carried the small creature and sat near Ryle. The kitten was gray with white splotches all over. It was scared curled up in her arms. "It's adorable," Ryle smiled as Aisha placed it on his lap. The kitten snuggled up in Ryle's arms; from her, it was terrified, Ryle noticed. "It's okay, little guy, you are safe with me," he caressed it's fur gently as Aisha admired it. "I think you should take it home rather than me," Aisha smiled. "How? I mean I haven't taken care of an animal before!" Ryle looked at Aisha with wide, confused eyes. "You will learn," She chuckled. "Who knows it might give you some company? I mean, what's the harm in it?" Ryle sighed, "As you say mam." He smiled as he got up. "I should be taking this little guy home," Aisha nodded as Ryle smiled. "Thank you for today," Ryle held the kitten and headed to his home. Aisha saw the dark-haired boy leave. He was too gentle for this world, the sweetest guy she ever met. She enjoyed his company, his comforting voice, gentle actions, and his kind heart were only some of his qualities. It caught her off guard, thinking about him. It made her wonder if was she in love.

Lessons Start

Aisha shrugged her thoughts away. She could not be in love with Ryle, they were just friends. Besides, Skye was her boyfriend. That was the person she was in love with. She let out a sigh and went home.

Eleonora took her brother to his room. She seemed disturbed, as if she was angered by someone or something. Silence filled the room. Skye didn't know what to say, he just kept looking down like he had done something wrong. "Brother, who did this?" Eleonora finally broke the silence looking into the hurt blonde's eyes. Skye tried to make up an excuse, but it was of no use. El already knew that behind this beastly behavior, there was none other than her brother's die-hard lover. "Skye, why do you stay with him? Look at yourself. Aren't you in pain? Why are you hurting yourself? Just leave him." Skye gently placed his index finger on his little sister's lips, "El no, I cannot leave him because I love him, you look at my wounds, but did you see the bandages over it?" Eleonora rolled her eyes. "He cleaned them up and took care of me the entire night. He might be abusive but El, he cares." Skye ran his hand through his sister's hair. He softly held her chin and made her look at him. "Your brother is going to be okay, I promise. Nothing can hurt me if you are okay," he smiled as Elenora hugged him tightly. She couldn't blame her brother.

Finally, he had found someone who would love him, someone who cared; even if he was abusive, at least he had a heart. Her brother had never got the affection he had longed for since he was a child and now that he was getting it, she didn't want to be the one who destroyed it. "Just take care of yourself for me. I wouldn't bear it if anything happened," Elenora held him tightly "If I won't be there, then who will care of this little monster?" They giggled as they fell asleep.

Ryle went home, holding the little creature in his hands. He didn't know how his father would react. To be honest, he didn't care. He hid the kitten inside his jacket and walked in. His father was lying on the couch as usual. Ryle crept up to his room and locked the door behind him. He placed the kitten down. "You must be hungry," he smiled. "Let me bring you something to eat. Don't move." The kitten tilted its head softly as Ryle left the room. The lad went to the kitchen and searched for a raw fish. He found it and took it to his room. To his terror, the kitten was nowhere to be found. "Meow meow" he looked around for the little beast. Ryle bent down and found the kitten hiding under his bed. "Come out, little guy, I'm not going to hurt you," he smiled softly as he pulled it out. He made the kitten sit on his lap and put the raw fish in front of it. "What's wrong? You don't like it?" The kitten just tilted its head. Ryle sighed, "Picky eater, aren't you?" He put the Kitten down and went out for a second time. Soon he returned with a bowl of milk. "Drink this," he said as he put the bowl of milk down. The kitten rushed to it, and drank it up. Ryle sat on his bed with satisfaction. He lay down, closing his eyes to sleep. Suddenly, his chest felt heavy. Was it the negative thoughts he was thinking or…. He opened his eyes, and he found the kitten sleeping on him. "No no! You sleep down." He picked it up and put it down. He laid back down. The kitten climbed up on his chest again. "Aish, sleep here. I am going to name you Aish, from Aisha," he smiled. "You just look like her. The same mischievous eyes and that stubbornness," he chuckled. "Good night," he smiled and fell asleep. The sun was nowhere to be seen. Monsoons were here. The teens were in their schools. The day passed quickly. Skye did not want to piss his dad off more, so he went home quickly. Ryle and Aisha walked alone. "So... we're going to my place?" Aisha looked down, waiting for an answer. "Yep, let's go," Ryle ruffed her hair "By the way, why have football lessons stopped?" Aisha wondered as it had been long since they had been to class, at least it felt long. "I guess, they do it because of the exams coming up. I am not quite sure though," Ryle replied. Aisha just nodded as they kept walking down the road. "What did you name the kitten?" she smiled, remembering their time together the day before. "Aish," Ryle smiled. "He has the same eyes as you. The same stubborn spirit as you," he chuckled. Aisha's lips curled into a smile. Ryle put his hand around Aisha's shoulder. "Yah! I am not that short okay," Aisha pouted as Ryle let out a laugh, "You wish!?" They walked together laughing and talking about various things. It was the ideal time they could spend together. Soon they reached. "First time I am coming through your front door huh?" Ryle chuckled as he realized that this was the first time he was going to Aisha's home and not sneaking in. Aisha hit him with her elbow as they stepped inside. "Mom, I'm home and I have a guest" Aisha yelled as her mom came out of the kitchen. "Hi," Aisha's mom smiled. "Hi, miss," Ryle bowed. "I am Ryle, Aisha's classmate. We decided to have a group study, so I came. I hope I'm not causing

Lessons Start

any trouble for you!" "Not at all" Aisha's mother smiled "You kids can go upstairs, and study. If you need anything call me." Aisha rolled her eyes on how overly polite Ryle was behaving. "Yes Mother," she gave a sarcastic smile as she grabbed Ryle's arm and took him upstairs. "You don't have to be that polite," the girl said in a mocking tone. "Just trying to give a pleasant impression, sweetheart," Ryle smiled as he set down on her bed. "Yea, yea," Aisha gave him a small pout. The teenagers opened their books and began studying. While reading, Ryle kept making up lame jokes and Aisha couldn't stop herself from laughing. Ryle loved to make her laugh. Seeing his world happy filled him up with love. It felt like every second he laid eyes on her, his love deepened; every second he looked at her, he fell deeper; every second his heart grew fonder. He held himself back as always with a smile on his face. "Let's take a break, I am tired," Aisha sighed as she lay on the bed to rest. "As you wish, I could use some rest," he smiled, sitting beside her. Silence filled the room as both relaxed on the soft mattress "Ryle, do you think our exams would go well?" Aisha looked worried now. Ryle caressed her hair "Don't worry" he smiled. "Everything will be okay, whether we struggle or not at the end of the day everything will be okay, trust me." Aisha smiled and looked at him "Thank you". She got up and opened her book again, "Let's continue or we will not be able to get over with it". Ryle nodded. They continued studying, it was late now. Ryle looked out the window wondering how Aish was. His eyes traveled back to Aisha. She was crouched near the book, reading out loud, her hair draped over her face as her hand rested on the edge of the book. She looked like a graceful deer who was bending down to drink water. His eyes gazed over the beautiful silhouette of the girl in front of him. Suddenly, he felt his heart start to race, his breathing got faster, and he couldn't control it. This had never happened before, so he didn't know how to react. His eyes now stared at Aisha's lips; he longed to kiss them. He moved in closer. It felt like his body was not in his control. It's wrong, it's wrong, it's wrong, he mumbled, his voice only audible to him. She was dating his friend; in fact, his best friend. He couldn't kiss her, he couldn't do it. He had always pulled himself back, but now could he do it? He looked up at Aisha's siren eyes that were innocently tracing the book. No, he couldn't do this, he couldn't do this to her. He pulled himself back and got up. "I need to go," he said in an ice-cold voice. Aisha looked at him confused, "Why do you have to go all of a sudden? Did anything happen?" Ryle looked away. "It's getting late," Ryle glanced back at her, her face forming a frown. "Thank you for today," he gave her a cold smile as he walked out of the room before rushing down the stairs. He was out in the cold on a lonely night. The boy looked up at the stars. Why was it always him who had to give up on people he loved? The one thing he needed the most was he didn't have a "human connection? He walked down a dimly lit street. Things would have been so different if his mother was here, but even she had given up on him. Even after accomplishing so much in his life, he felt like a failure. He let out a deep sigh. He closed his eyes and thought about Aisha and Skye. They were his family; they were his home. His lips turned into a smile. Even if Aisha was not his, he was grateful just to be near her. The boy desperately tried to find something good in his life. He knew he just needed to hold strong, he had faith that time changes everything. He went home and was greeted by a drunk father, who was lying on the couch.. Ryle sighed as he ran his hand through his hair and went into his room. Aish came meowing towards Ryle as Ryle picked him up in his arms "Hey little guy, missed me, did you?" He smiled as Aish snuggled in his arms. He went to the kitten and poured some milk for Aish as he drank it up satisfied. Ryle went and lay on his bed. Aish followed him and lay on his left arm. "Can't sleep without me, can you?" Ryle chuckled as he laid on his side and hugged Aish. Good night little one," he said as he closed his eyes. There was only one thing bothering him. Today he held himself back from kissing Aisha, but if in the same situation again, would he do it?

Home

$\mathcal{S}$aturday morning the sun rose. The bright sunlight hit Aisha's face; she yawned and sat up straight. Her hair was a mess, and she could barely open her eyes. She rubbed her eyes and stretched her back. Her room was filled with books from yesterday's study. She remembered the previous day and a smile unwillingly formed her face. Suddenly she had an idea, she called both Skye and Ryle and told them to meet her behind the school. Aisha struggled with being punctual so to no one's surprise, she arrived late. "Look who decided to show up," Ryle chuckled. "Early? Aren't you miss Aisha?" Skye smiled and hugged her. "I am so sorry guys, I took time getting ready," the brunette giggled. "It's okay, though what happened all of a sudden and you called us on a Saturday morning?" Ryle wondered. Aisha put her hands on her waist, "I have a plan!" she exclaimed. "Tell us miss what is your master plan!" Skye mimicked her actions. "So, as you guys know there is an amusement park nearby that recently opened. I was thinking maybe we could go there and spend a day together! Please don't say no, you guys are my only friends," Aisha whined. "Sure!" Ryle said with a smile. Skye seemed skeptical, he looked away, lost in his thoughts. Aisha clung onto Ryle's arms "Yahh! Ryler please convince your friend! Pleaseee," Aisha whined as Ryle let out a sigh. "Skye c'mon. It is one day; it can't hurt you. For us, please,"

Ryle smiled. Skye rolled his eyes, "Fine, but just this once." The teens cheered. They headed towards the amusement park. The sun shone bright, and the leaves danced to the music of the wind. Aisha easily got distracted by a butterfly soaring through the air. Ryle held her arm. "Stay, we don't need to be late, do we?" he smiled. The trio finally arrived. The amusement park was huge. There were all sorts of carnival rides. Big, small, colorful- it was like a dreamland. A big mile plastered on Aisha's face. Ryle looked at her as her eyes. glistened. "What are you guys waiting for? Let's go," Aisha took the lead as she ran ahead. "My treat," Skye smiled as he paid for the tickets. The teens decided to go on the ferris wheel. Not too fast, not too slow, they got on the ride as it started. The shining bright sun got replaced with dark clouds. Skye smiled at the dark clouds as they reminded him of Alex. They were dark and cold, just like Alex was but they and had a weird comfort to them. Just like his lover had. The blonde boy looked at his friend and said "lover". As they reached the top, Aisha looked down. She put her hands on the caged door as she bent down to see the tiny city better. Ryle slid his hand around her waist. His grip was tight and he had her in place. Aisha felt his cold hand slither around her waist. Her short top allowed her to feel every one of his touches. He came close to her ear as she felt his warm breath on her neck "Be careful," the dark-haired boy whispered. Aisha nodded as she smiled. She felt weird butterflies in her stomach. She didn't want to feel that way. Skye was lost in his world. He looked down and admired the city. Soon the ride came to a stop. The teens decided to go have some ice cream. "What flavor do you guys want?" Ryle asked as he clenched the money in his pocket. "The best flavor there is, chocolate!" Asha giggled. Skye scoffed "Mint chocolate is the best flavor!" "Ah you guys and your couple fights," Ryle facepalmed as he went inside. Skye and Aisha found a place to sit as they waited for Ryle. Skye held Aisha's hand on her lap, embracing it softly. Ryle came and handed them their ice creams. "How's study going, guys?" Skye asked as he fed Aisha her ice-cream "Good, I guess," Ryle poked his ice cream as he picked a bite and shoved it into his mouth. Aisha nodded. "What about you? I am sure you're going to pass with amazing grades. You always do," Aisha caressed his hand. "I guess so, but I miss you guys sometimes," He genuinely had fun with Aisha and Ryle. They were his world besides Alex. Aisha giggled as she stood up, "No more talks about studies. Let's go to the roller coaster." The two boys stood and walked with her. She grabbed their heads and their heads locked both on each side. "I love being with you guys!" she giggled as she let them go. Ryle chuckled, "Us too, I suppose" he winked at Skye, Skye nodded as they made their way to the roller coaster. Skye gulped. "This is the thing you want to ride?" Skye stammered. Ryle smirked as he grabbed Skye's arms "You can't chicken out now!" The teens Sat on the tremble-worthy ride. Skye sat with Ryle as Aisha sat alone. "I can't wait!" Aisha squealed, excited in her seat. Skye trembled as Ryle teased him. The ride started. It was as fast as lightning. Skye was horrified; he screamed his lungs out. Meanwhile, Ryle and Aisha were having the time of their lives. The ride soon ended as the teens got off. Aisha was jumping around wheezing, mumbling about how fun the ride was. No one could understand her as she was too excited but seeing her happy Ryle smiled. Skye was a mess as Ryle helped him walk. "That was hell," Skye muttered. "Oh come on, Mr. negative, it wasn't that bad," Ryle teased him. Skye smiled as seeing his friends happy made him happy. They were his family, his world. The teens hung around for the rest of the day.

They enjoyed it. Aisha missed this time with her friends. They made her happy, they were the reason for her happiness. The day soon ended as the teens walked home. "Thanks to both of you for coming today you made my day" Aisha smiled. "It's nothing, darling," Skye kissed the back of her hand as Ryle nodded. They were her new friends; they were the ones. As the sun set, Aisha reached home. The stars shone bright as she bid them goodbye. She leaned on her front door as she watched them walk away. She smiled remembering the memorable day she had spent. Finally, she had found her people, her family from her, her home.

Gone Wrong

*I*t was Monday evening; school was over and Aisha and Ryle were walking together. The sun was setting, both were having a tiring day. As exams were near, the professors had given them loads of work.

"I kind of miss having football lessons. I miss being with you and Skye," Aisha hugged Ryle's arm "Don't worry. Soon this will also end. At least I can stay with you. Without you, I would fail." It was true that Aisha had helped Ryle study. She helped him concentrate; she helped him learn. Ryle used to tease her, saying she could become a teacher, but she always denied it as it seemed too boring to her. As they reached, they got comfortable on Aisha's bed. It was usual for them now; it had become their everyday routine. It was time to study math, and Ryle hated math. Aisha opened her books as the teens started to study. Ryle couldn't understand anything. The brunette took pauses and gave emphasis to the things that Ryle couldn't quite understand. Even after so many tries, Ryle just seemed lost. He stared at Aisha, the way she was analyzing things. Ryles was mesmerized by her beauty. He didn't know what to do. The harder he tried to take his eyes off her the more he was attracted. "Let's take a break!" Aisha broke the silence; the dark-haired boy gulped, and nodded. "Control Yourself Ryller, for Skye," he held himself back. After a while, the teens resumed their studies. Aisha noticed that Ryle was uneasy though she couldn't understand why. Aisha put her hand on Ryle's thigh and looked into his eyes "Hey, are you okay?" Ryle looked into her eyes. He felt hypnotized by her touch, her beauty. He just stared into her eyes before he softly nodded. Aisha leaned towards Ryle getting closer to him. Ryle felt the heat between them. Their faces were one inch away from each other. They stared into each other's eyes. Aisha started to breathe heavily; she held Ryle's thigh tighter. Ryle realized there was no turning back now, he was about to go against everything he stood for. The dark-haired boy didn't have time to think more; he felt Aisha's warm lips pushed against his. Aisha's lips were warm, comforting just like lukewarm water before entering the bathtub. In contrast, Ryle's lips were cold, almost numb…! With their lips now connected, both teens shut their eyes. Ryle removed all the obstacles between them. as he pulled the girl on his lap. Their bodies clashed and smashed against each other. They had longed to be there, they had longed to touch each other, to hold each other. Aisha wrapped her arms around Ryle's neck, deepening the kiss, her thighs squeezing against the boy's slim but worked-out waist. Ryle's hands held Aisha's hair, caressing them, and holding them. Their bodies had chemistry. Ryle's hands traveled down to her waist pulling her closer. Ryle bit her lower lip as it started to bleed. He sucked! the blood relieving her of her pain. They felt hypnotized, like someone was controlling them. Aisha's eyes shot open she realized what she was doing. She immediately pushed Ryle and got off him. "I'm sorry," the boy muttered as he sat up straight. "What's wrong with me?" Aisha spat out as she held her head. Ryle got up. "This means nothing, just so you know. I am leaving." "Don't put the blame on me, Ryle!" Aisha desperately tried to defend herself. Ryle let out a sigh as he walked out, what had he just done...? Aisha fell to her knees. Tears filled her eyes. She regretted her actions. To be honest, she regretted going behind Skye's back, not kissing Ryle. Negative thoughts filled her head. Ryle didn't want her. Not only did she lose Ryle but Skye too. She lost her family, her friends, her home. Not again, not again, the girl started panicking. She lay on her bed and stuck her head on a pillow. She just sobbed; there was nothing she could do now.

Ryle walked home, he felt exhausted. He was disappointed in himself, how could he do this to Skye, his best friend? He took a stop near a park. The lad was guilty of what he had just done. He patted his pocket in search of "it". Ryle took the pack out. He slid a cigarette out of the pack. It had been a long time since he had last smoked. Everyone has a coping mechanism, whether it is listening to music, bathing, going for a walk or even harming yourself. Some coping mechanisms are worse than others, and so was Ryle's. He just harmed himself; but I guess a coping mechanism is a coping mechanism. Ryle lit the cigarette on fire as he took a puff. The toxic "air" burned his lungs, but he didn't care. He just wanted to feel the pain, he felt like he deserved it. The sun had set; it was night now. Ryle looked around the dead streets with numb eyes. Ryle's mother had died when the lad was young. The boy always felt like his mother had left him all alone in this monstrous world. His thoughts had always put him down; no one ever believed in him except Aisha and Skye. He smiled at the thought of them but now he had lost them. There goes his everything. Ryle gritted his teeth; he felt angry and disappointed in everything and everyone. He sighed as he walked the dark alleyway. The cigarette burnt out. Ryle threw it on the ground as he stamped on it. He didn't care about littering the area. This was the last thing he could be cautious about... Ryle stood in front of his hell of a house. The lad threw his head back as he took a deep breath. He closed his eyes as he breathed in from his nose and out from his mouth. The dark-haired boy ruffled his hair as he stepped into the house. Out of nowhere he heard yelling and banging noises. They were coming from his room, though he didn't understand why. Then it hit him, Aish was in that room! Ryle ran to his room, almost falling off the stairs.

Why Me?

Ryle was panicking. What if something had happened to the poor creature? What if he was too late? Ryle barged into his room just to find his "father" yelling at the kitten that was hidden under his bed. "Dad! Let it go, I am here now. I can take care of it please." His father reeked of alcohol. A Smell he hated since he was a kid. A smell that always surrounded his father. His father looked at him with burning eyes. "You!" he grabbed the dark-haired boy by the collar, "How dare you bring this wretched thing into my house !?" He shook the boy as Ryle shut his eyes. He was in no mood to deal with this monster. "Answer me!" the man roared in the boy's ears. "I am going to keep him in the room, I don't think it will create problems. Please," Ryle had to reason peacefully. Ryle always tried to be reasonable as he hated conflict, but he never seemed able to do it with his father. "That thing is a damn curse I tell you, a curse!" the older man yelled. Ryle sighed at the drunk man's idiotic comments. He needed a hug but instead, he was here dealing with the burden of a father. "Dad stop with those superstitions. You know that it's rot," Ryle's fathers stroked the boy across his face. "You dare to talk back, you little shit!" Ryle just looked down, not moving an inch. If you won't, I will get rid of it," the beast walked towards Ryle's bed. "No, he wouldn't." The monster reached his hand out and pulled the little angel out of its hiding spot. The stranger's aggressive touch made the kitten hiss in pain. The man held the kitten tightly in his palm as he lifted his hand and threw it on the floor. They say cats have nine lives but that was just a little kitten. It didn't know how to land on its feet yet. Its little body smashed on the floor with a loud THUD. It didn't even make a sound, it didn't move. It just lay there with shut eyes. Ryle felt horrified. He didn't recognize this monster in front of him. His father had beaten him since he was young, he did not care but this was inhuman. Ryle lost his cool he lunged at his father, grabbing him by his collar. The older man was shocked by the boy's reaction. Ryle's eyes were fuming with anger. He had nothing but hatred inside of him. Ryle's hand turned into a fist as he rained punches on his father's face. All these years he suffered, he stayed with that monster for years. The anger he had locked up in his chest lashed out. The boy had turned into a heartless demon. It was back in time; Ryle was just 5 years old. Back then his mom was still alive. She took Ryle, she loved him unconditionally. "Ryle, darling, wake up," his mom took the 5-year-old in her arms of her as she cuddled him. The boy opened his eyes softly as he held onto his mother's arm. "I don't want to get up. I want to stay," the sleepy boy mumbled, as he adjusted himself in her arms. The lady chuckled as he patted Ryle's cheek. "I don't want my baby boy to be late," she smiled as the sleepy child sat in her arms. She got Ryle ready for kindergarten, his father was at work. They walked to the kindergarten together. Ryle held his mother's hand as they walked, his mother's hand was warm and comforting. She made him feel safe. As they reached Ryle burst into tears. His mom knelt to his level and wiped the sobbing boy's eyes. "Why are you crying, baby boy?" her sweet voice echoed in his ears. "Y--you are l-leaving me," the boy managed to say between his sobs. His mom gave him a charming smile. "I can never leave my prince, it's just a matter of a few hours. I will be back to pick you up soon," she caressed his black hair. The boy sniffed with a tiny pout. "Promise?" She held his arms and kissed him on the forehead. "Before you know it mama will be back to pick you up, I promise." The boy hugged her as she caressed his hair. It was evening. Ryle's mother loves to pick him up. "Honey, you want me to go pick him up?" Ryle's father said, hugging her by her waist. Back then, he wasn't a drunkard. He was a caring father and a wonderful husband. "I promised him that I would go and pick him up. I should go now!" She kissed his cheek as she left. The sun was about to set as she rushed to pick him up. She was worried that Ryle would think that she forgot him Ryle was an extremely sensitive kid that was affected by everything. She smiled at that thought of her little angel. She was one street away as she ran to cross the street, she saw Ryle who waved at her from across the street. She couldn't wait to hold her son in her arms. A bus honking sound echoed in her ears as she saw a flashing light. Tremendous pain filled her body as it hit the ground. She heard a little kid yell and Ryle leaning over her. That was the last thing she saw. Days later, her funeral took place, and Ryle was numb. He just stared emotionlessly at his mom's casket. His entire family was there. The "family" that in future never stood for him, never cared for him; they didn't even think about him. The boy was left all alone. As her casket was being buried, the boy screamed and yelled. "You can't leave me alone mama," he sobbed "You promised! Come back," he cried and hit his little arms in the air, but it was of use. "She is in a better place," said the priest; he was the only one who comforted him. After that day, his father started drinking. He used Ryle as a punching bag, nothing more. That was his worth. Ryle's mother never left him but that's how he always felt. She left him all alone with that monster. From a loving father, he had become a hideous monster. Ryle's father got money as he used to be a government worker, but he always gambled it away or spent it on alcohol. The boy used to cry at night, he missed his mother. After his mother's death, he promised himself that he will never be weak again, he could never depend on anybody. Ryle's eyes shot open with rage. He continued raining punches on the older man in front of him. The man struggled under his sons grip. He didn't expect Ryle to be this strong. He had always seen his son as a weak lad who couldn't stand up for himself. Ryle seemed like a different person or maybe a person he never noticed changed. Ryle stopped as he stared at his father. That wasn't his father, he was an unrecognizable monster who was somehow related to him. Ryle's eyes fell on the still-unconscious kitten. His anger came rushing back to his head. The poor creature didn't deserve it. The man raised his hand to slap Ryle, but Ryle caught his arm. They stared at each other dead in the eyes. Ryle's grip on him tightened around his father's arm. There was rage, fire in his eyes. His father saw his sweet, loving little boy turning into a heartless demon and it was all because of him. Ryle raised his arm and punched the man's jaw making him fall to the ground, "Ryle c-calm d..down I w-we can sort this!" the man cried out in hopes of calming the boy down. It was of no use; all these years Ryle had been enduring so much and today was the end of it. He grabbed the man by his collar, shaking him mercilessly. "What is wrong with you!? All these years why did you hurt me! I was your son, you monster, why did hurt me !?" The boy roared, letting all his emotional pain out.

Aisha was panicking. Why wasn't he replying to her? Did she mess up that bad? Was he with Skye? Aisha couldn't help but overthink. She was worried, she couldn't stand the thought of losing Ryle and Skye. How could she after everything they had been through together? She grabbed her phone and sneaked out of her balcony. Her mother would not let her out that late and she knew it. That's why she preferred to sneak out even if there was a chance that she could get in trouble. She was ready to risk everything for them. She walked down the dark roads on her own. It was dangerous but her safety was the last thing she cared about. She reached near Ryle's house as she heard him yelling. She panicked. Was Ryle in trouble? Did his father hurt him again? She remembered seeing his bruises from him and being horrified. She couldn't stand the thought of Ryle being in pain. She rushed towards Ryle's house The door was unlocked. She looked around. The stench of alcohol hit her nose. How could Ryle live here? She heard someone yell from upstairs. She ran up the stairs. panicking, thinking about all the possible things that could be going on. She barged in the door. The sight of her in front of her made her feel horrified. Ryle's father was knocked down to the ground as Ryle aggressively held him by his collar. Ryle shook him, screaming in his face. Ryle looked like another person. He was not his sweet but cold and loving self of him, he was a heartless beast. The kitten was lying unconscious in the corner of the room. Aisha connected the dots. Ryle was such a mess that he didn't notice Aisha entering the room. Aisha rushed over and picked up the injured kitten in her arms, shaking it gently in hopes of waking it up. "You bastard. You never cared about your son! You heartless beast!" He started to punch his father with all his force. The man started to bleed but Ryle couldn't care less. "Ryle enough, he is bleeding. You should stop now," Aisha cried out. Ryle was surprised by her presence, but he did not care. "No, Aisha. All these years I suffered because of him, now it's my turn!" he yelled as he swung his arms and hit the man in front of him. "Ryle, no! That's what makes you better than him… you are not a monster." Ryle let the man go as his body hit the floor. Ryle sighed and ran his hand through his hair. "Get out of my house." Ryle looked at the man. The man's eyes widened as he stood up. "Ryle no, we can work this out," he tried calming his son down. "Get out!" the boy grabbed the man by the collar as he dragged him down the stairs and pushed him out the door. "Ryle, you will regret this," the man tried to protest. "I hope I do," Ryle slammed the door on his face. The boy stood with his back to the door and aggressively wiped his tears before running upstairs.

Skye was out with Alex. The two boys were in the school field embracing each other. The boys chuckled and kissed. Skye could never get enough of his lover "Baby boy it's time, you need to head home," Alex caressed the boys' hair. "I don't want to!" Skye protested Alex stood up and lifted the boy off his feet "I will take you home so be a good boy and obey," he chuckled and kissed his boy's temple. The boys walked to Skye's home giggling and talking about each other. They genuinely loved being with each other. They finally reached Skye's home as they gave each other a fist bump as a goodbye. "Why is he with his friend at this hour?" Skye's father talked as he watched them through the window. They had no idea they were being watched. Skye hugged

Alex as a last goodbye, but Alex had other plans. He grabbed the blond's golden hair pulling them aggressively behind as he joined their lips. He bit Skye's lip as blood trickled down and the boy whimpered. Skye's father watched in horror as he finally figured it out.

Reality

The boy dashed upstairs. What was Aisha going through? Was the kitten ultimately okay? Or did she…. Ryle brushed his thoughts away as he went into his room. He saw Aisha sitting on the floor holding his kitten in her arms. Tears rolled down her face as the kitten wasn't moving. Ryle let out a sigh as he went and sat near her. "Hey, it's okay. I am sorry this was all because of me, I should have taken better care of him." A tear rolled down his cheek as he quickly wiped it. "No, Ryle, don't blame yourself. There was nothing you could do," she struggled to hold her tears back. She placed the little kitten on the bed as she hugged Ryle. "You have gone through a lot tonight. I hope you are okay." She broke the hug and looked at him. Ryle smiled softly. Even after everything, she had the strength to care about him. To question his feelings. Ryle caressed her hair as his hand traveled down to her cheek and then her chin. He held her chin gently as he made her look into his eyes. "I am fine Aisha, I am sorry you had to see all this today. You shouldn't have come." The boy was guilty as he blamed himself for Aisha being sad. "Don't say that!" She joined her forehead with his. "I am glad I came, and you weren't alone. It's good to know someone has your back," she smiled softly. The teens closed their eyes as they stood with their joined foreheads. They both felt safe and comfortable. From the corner of her eye, Aisha saw something move. She immediately turned toward the kitten. "It moved!" she shot up and picked Aish up. The girl caressed it's gray fur, shaking it softly. The gray angel slowly opened his eyes. "Yes! Ryle, Aish is okay!" the teens cheered. "You gave us a scare, buddy," Ryle rejoiced as the kitten got up. They were more than happy to know that no permanent harm was done. The kitten lay on Aisha's lap as now everything was good. Aisha looked at the smiling dark-haired boy. She had longed to see him happy. "So, what do you plan on doing with your father?" she asked in a soft voice as she took hold of his hand and made him pet the kitten. Ryle shrugged his shoulders. "What's left to do now? He will be no part of my life anymore." Ryle was emotionless while talking about his father. I wonder how much he had suffered because of him. "Whatever you need, I am always here," she said as she looked at him and smiled. "Even when the stars and moon collide, I will always be there by your side, forever and ever" Ryle admired her. How could she love a damaged person so much, he thought. It wasn't possible to love a person like him and yet she proved him wrong. The girl leaned in closer to his face while looking into his eyes. "This time it's not a mistake," she kissed him.

Alex wiped the blood off his lover's chin. "I love you," he kissed Skye's eyes. Skye smiled, "Me more". The boy bid his goodbye as he swiftly walked into the door. Skye had done it many times and he never got in trouble. He thought everyone was asleep as he closed the door behind him. "Welcome home," a familiar voice thundered behind him. Skye's heart dropped. He turned round and saw his father. Skye's feet trembled. Did his dad see him? Does he know now? Skye couldn't help but stutter

"Hey d-dad". His father had a look of disappointment and anger on his face. "Come in the living room," his father said with a numb voice. Skye did not know what to say. The blonde was terrified. The lad knew nothing but to obey. He nodded softly as he went and sat on the couch. Skye's legs were trembling he put his hand on his knee to stop it from shaking. His father looked like a tyrant. His father bit the inside of his cheek as he stared at the boy from head to toe with a disgusted expression. Silence filled the air. Skye looked at his feet trying not to panic. Skye's father broke the silence, "Since when has this been going on?" The man got up and walked towards the shaking lad. "What has been going on?" The boy managed to spit out. "You fucking that boy?" Skye's father thundered as he stroked him across the face. Skye was left speechless. His cheek burnt but he didn't care. His secret was out, everything was over now. Skye teared up. The tears were not because of pain in his cheek, but out of the fear of losing Alex. Eleonora and Skye's mother woke up from all the screaming as they rushed down. "What's going on?" Skye's mother asked as she went down the stairs with her daughter. Skye's father scoffed looking at his son, "He didn't tell you? Your son is fucking gay," he yelled. Eleorona's hands covered her mouth. No…her brother's secret was out. She couldn't believe it. Her father wouldn't let it go lightly and she knew it. Skye's mother looked at him with disgust. "Not only that, you know he has been fucking another boy behind our back," he stroked Skye again. The boy trembled. He wanted Alex. He needed Alex. The had longed to be hugged, comforted accepted above all loved…Alex was his everything; now he was going to lose him. His father grabbed him by his arm and shook him, "What didn't we give you? How could you do this to us?" he yelled. He made Skye feel like it was his fault like he was someone bad, someone different. Skye's tears trickled down his sore cheeks. "Dad enough, he heard it," as always, his sister tried to stand up for him. She was the only one who loved him and that was his sad reality. Skye's father looked at her with blood-shot eyes. "Elenora, you know about it!?" he yelled, making Skye flinch at every word. Elenora just looked down saying nothing. Skye didn't want her to be in trouble because of him. It was his mess, and he couldn't get her in trouble. "No, she didn't know about me. I am sorry," Skye mustered up the courage and spoke. Skye's dad scoffed, "Learn something from her." He grabbed Skye's arm and made him stand. Skye didn't want to look at his sister. He knew her sadness could tear his heart apart. "I will take care of him," Skye's father glared at the blonde. Skye knew his dad had an evil plan in mind. The lad wanted the ground to open and swallow him up. His dad tightened his grip around the lad's arm. He aggressively pulled Skye and dragged him upstairs pushing him into his room. "You will be going to a boarding school they will set you straight. I will make sure you never see that boy, or your friends ever again. Mind my words." The door banged and clicked as his father locked him in the room.

Skye's heart stopped racing. He felt numb, he wished that day never existed. His heart sank to his stomach. A sickness filled up my body. Every second his chest felt heavier. He felt his blood run cold. "No no, this can't be happening, tell me it's a joke," were the only things the lad could blurt out. Tears flooded his eyes but none of them dropped. "You can't do this to me make me happy then snatch it away from me." The boy's thoughts were hurting him. He felt nauseous so he got up and went to his bathroom. He just stared at himself in the mirror, and calmed himself down.

He had to lie on his bed and tried to distract himself, though he couldn't focus on anything. "Just tell me it's a lie, I beg you," were his last thoughts before he lost his strength to think.

Aisha broke the kiss as she smiled staring at her lover, she placed the kitten on a pillow as Ryle made her sit on his lap. He placed his hand on her thigh caressing it softly. She let herself relax in her arms. His body heat covered her and kept her warm. "I love you," the dark-haired boy muttered, holding her in his arms. "I love you too," the girl smiled but soon her smile faded Ryle noticed it, he always noticed her emotions. "What's wrong?" He caressed her arm. "I feel bad for going behind Skye's back..." She looked down sadly. Ryle chuckled. "It's time you know the truth," Ryle made her sit straight on his lap Aisha looked at him with confusion.

The Truth

Ryle caressed her silky and messy hair. Aisha looked like a dream. A dream that he thought would never come true, but it was reality "Ryle, tell me," The girl said as Ryle snapped out of his thoughts. "Oh yes," the boy cleared his throat. "See, Skye is my best friend and I had to keep this hidden some things are better unsaid, and many times there is no other way." Ryle sighed as he knew that what he was about to say wouldn't be that easy for her to accept. Ryle caressed his lover's thigh trying to comfort her as she held onto his arm. Aisha wanted to say something, but she held herself back. She wanted to hear the whole truth. "Skye never loved you… he never felt anything towards you Aisha." Those harsh words slipped Ryle's mouth. Aisha couldn't believe it. "How is that possible"?. "He loves someone else" Ryle continued, "Then why did he stay with me? He could have just told me," Aisha scoffed. She felt angry and her emotions were justified. She had lived in darkness all along; Ryle cupped her cheeks and made her look at him. "It's Alex, Skye is in relation with Alex" Aisha was left speechless. She didn't know what to say or how to react. "You were the only way he could date Alex, or his parents would suspect him. You know what good of an image his parents demand. The boy had no other option. So, if you want to get mad at him, you can. Just know he never meant any harm," Ryle let go of her. The girl stayed silent, she tried to think through everything that Ryle said. Of course, it wasn't easy for her, but it was already done, right? There was nothing she could do now. "If you want to be mad at him, just remember I am a culprit too. The only thing I ask of you is to not tell anyone. I can't let you do that." Ryle looked away. He was a good friend and under no circumstance he could let Skye get into trouble. Skye had been there for him and now it was his turn. Despite the unconditional love for Aisha, he couldn't let her do that. Aisha smiled at the boy's words. She held Ryle's cheeks as she made him look at her. "Ryller, I could never be mad at Skye for that, let alone think about exposing him. I couldn't do that to him. No matter our differences, he always stood by me, and I have the best memories with him," she caressed Ryle's hair. "Plus, he and Alex make a good couple." The teens giggled. Ryle admired Aisha. He had never met a person as understanding as her. He loved her more than anything. "I love you, Aisha. I love you so much," he looked into her eyes as she pecked his lips. "I love you more."

"You two, go to bed, I will deal with the boy later," Skye's father said as he came from Skye's room. Eleanora didn't know how to act. The girl was worried for her brother. She didn't know what she could do at that point. She went to her room. The girl held her tears back. It wasn't the time to cry. She had to do something. But what? That was the only thing traumatizing her. She knew her father would do something, but she didn't know what. She lay on her bed, thinking about what her brother would be going through. The night soon passed as the girl couldn't sleep. It was around four in the morning when she sneaked into her brother's room. She knocked on the door. "Skye? Are you good in there?" she whispered in a soft voice. The boy heard his sister's voice as he rushed and put his ear on the door. "What are you doing here!? Leave at once Eleonora! What if Dad came huh? Leave," Skye replied in a worried tone. He was glad that Eleonora had come but he didn't want her to get in trouble. "I just came to check up upon you," she struggled between her tears. "Hey El, I am okay, I promise. Go to your room and rest. I will be okay, don't cry. Now be a good girl for your big brother and listen to me, okay?" the blonde tried to comfort her. "I will, I will, big brother." She let her tears flow. "Take care please. I promise soon this will be over. I love you." She got up and ran to her room as she couldn't cry in front of her brother. Tears flowed down Skye's cheeks. He sat near his bed, crying into a pillow. He couldn't help but think how everyone would be happier without him. His friends would not have a burden anymore, his sister would not have to suffer, and Alex of course could find someone better. Thoughts like this tormented him. They made him feel so worthless. He just wished he could feel better. The more he tried pushing his thoughts away the louder they got. Skye held his head sobbing out loud. He wanted these monsters to get out of his head. He couldn't take it anymore. He felt so alone, he felt like he meant nothing anymore. He felt hated by all the people he loved. All that the boy wanted was a hug. Just to feel loved and safe. He cried and cried but nothing would change. He hated being alive at that moment. He struggled not to hurt himself. He just sobbed and sobbed with no outcome. The boy felt tired as he lay on his bed. He just wished this would end. He lay there, and even tried to cry at that point. The boy closed his eyes and drifted to his dreamland; the only place where he felt safe at that point. Life is a mess sometimes. The only thing you can do is wait for things to get better. Just don't make impulse decisions. Remember things always change.

Eleonora heard her father talking on the phone. She couldn't care less about the man's job. That's when she heard Skye's name. The girl panicked. She slowly opened her room's door, so she could hear what they were talking about. "Yea, I will bring him in on Monday. I just want you to set the lad straight," her father laughed. His laughter was so fake and disgusting. Eleonora hated that man more than anyone at that point. "A military camp is all the boy needs". Eleonora gasped. "No...." her brother was going to be sent to a military camp. He couldn't possibly survive it. It was Sunday which meant her brother would be going the next day. Eleonora couldn't let that happen. She had to do something to save her brother.

Help!

Eleonora felt helpless at that point. She was lost in her thoughts of her. She could not afford to lose her brother. He was her only family. As the girl lay on her bed, tears pooled in her eyes. She loved her brother more than anyone. Skye and Elenora had a close bond. He had practically raised the girl. Their parents were unavailable since they were young. Skye had dealt with a lot of negligence when he was a child, so he did not want his sister to go through the same thing. He always took over the role of his father and mother and took care of her as if she were his kin. Eleonora fought back her tears. She clenched the new pillow tightly in her arms. She shut her eyes tightly, remembering all her memories with her brother. Back in time when Elenora was young, she used to have nightmares. The girl always craved to go to her mom but to no surprise, her mom did not care. Eleonora woke up crying in her room. She was horrified after a horrible nightmare. The girl sobbed as the room got darker and scarier. The blond passed by the girl's room and heard her crying. That was a sound that he couldn't endure. The boy crept up and sat on her bed. "El? are you okay?" he said in a soft voice, trying not to scare her. The girl just sobbed. She crawled softly and sat on his lap hugging him and burying her face in his chest. Skye caressed her back as he picked her up. He thought it would be better if she slept with him. He cradled the young Child, trying to calm it down. "Enough sweetheart, you are safe now. I will let no one hurt my princess. You trust me, right?" the lad tried to be as sweet as possible. The terrified younger child nodded. He pat her back until she calmed down and laid with her on his chest. "Thank you, big bro," she mumbled in a trembling voice. Skye chuckled at his little sister. "Why didn't you come to me, darling? You know that I will always protect you," Skye said, caressing her blonde hair. She looked just like him just a younger and a female version. He saw himself in her, that was the reason he felt close to her, he couldn't see her in pain. The little girl looked up at him with her big doe eyes. Her gaze was innocent, she held his shirt in a small fist and softly pouted. "Mama told me not to disturb anyone when I am not feeling well," the kid teared up. "Sorry." Skye was quick to wipe her tears from her. "That bitch," he mumbled and looked back at her. "Ignore her, love. She speaks for herself not me. I will always be with you." The lad planted a small kiss on her forehead. Eleonora giggled to his touch "Bitch!" the girl spat out while laughing. "Yah! Don't say that it's a bad word," Skye corrected her. "Bitch!" the girl giggled again. Skye facepalmed himself. "Sleep now, it's getting late," he smiled and pat her back. The girl snuggled in his chest and soon drifted to her dreamland. Eleonora and Skye had been close since they were little kids. They were family and would do anything for each other.

Eleonora sat up straight and wiped her tears. She needed to do something. That's when it comes to her, she could go to Alex! The girl knew that on Sundays Alex used to practice football on the school's field. She remembered how Skye used to talk about him. Alex was the only one who could help her. The girl grabbed her phone and ran down the stairs. "I am going out with my friends," the girl yelled as she dashed out the door. She ran to the school field. She tried not to tear up, thinking about how she would convince Alex. What if she didn't find him? What if he did not want to come? She shrugged her thoughts away as she reached. She saw a tall man with brown hair playing football. He was on his own, So Elenora thought that was Alex. She went up to him trying to regain her senses and gain some confidence. The boy saw her and smiled. "Hey, are you okay?" the boy bent down to her level and held her forearm. She nodded with closed eyes and soon looked up at him. "Are you Alex?" she looked at him eyes full of desperation. The lad nodded. "Yes, what do you need?". "Skye is in trouble. Father found out about you and him and has locked him in his room. Skye will be sent to a military camp tomorrow and I am sure he could not make it out there. Please do something about it. You are the only one who can help me," the girl teared up. "He is the only one I have. He loves you and trusts you. You are the only one I can turn to," the girl managed to speak between her sobs. Alex froze in horror. He could not believe his ears. He held the sobbing girl by her arms and shook her. "Who are you and how do you know this!?" he asked aggressively. Tears flew down Eleonora's eyes. "I am Eleonora, his sister," she sobbed. Alex was taken aback. How did his father find out? Did anyone tell him, or did he see them? There was no time to think about this, he had to think of a plan. He saw the crying girl and sighed. He pulled her towards him, and he hugged her. The kid clung onto him in need of comfort. "He is going to be okay. We will do something about it." He caressed her back as she cried on his chest. "Hey, little one, enough," Alex struggled to speak in a soft tone. The way the girl acted was exactly like her brother. That's the reason he had spoken to her in a kind tone since the beginning. It suddenly hit him. "How much time do we have? Tell me," he said while caressing the girl's hair. "They are leaving tonight," the girl sobbed and held the older boy tighter. Alex gritted his teeth. He pulled the girl away from him and made her look in his eyes. The lad had an idea. It is hard when you are in trouble of course but it isn't harder when someone you love is in an uncomfortable place. When you are the only one, they can depend on. It's hard but that's when your instincts finally work. "Go down the road, and on the fifth street turn left. Knock on the second house and ask for Aisha. Explain everything to her and bring her here. Tell her Alex called," the lad gave precise details. How could he know so much and know the exact placement of everything, Eleonora thought. She had so many questions but now was not the time. She nodded as Alex wiped her tears, "Stay strong for your brother."

Elenora nodded and ran towards the street Alex had told her to go to. Alex knew exactly where Aisha and Ryle lived as they constantly used to hang out with them. In case anything happened, he had memorized both of their addresses. He reached Ryle's house and banged on the front door. He did not care if Ryle would get mad or if someone else opened the door. It was an emergency. He couldn't lose Skye. Skye was his everything. Except Ryle and Aisha, Alex knew no one who could help him. He could not do it alone with a little girl. He needed help, he needed someone to rely on, someone to help him with everything. Alex heard the front door open as he took a deep breath and got himself ready. Ryle was the only person Alex respected as a captain. The only person Alex could listen to. Ryle rubbed his eyes looking at Alex. "Alex! Is everything ok?" Ryle looked concerned. "Nothing is ok. I know that you know about me and Skye," Ryle got serious. "His father found out and is sending him to a military camp. You need to help me. His sister had gone to bring Aisha. Alex looked down. Ryle's eyes widened. "They are leaving tonight we need to do something," Alex pleaded. Ryle went inside and came back quickly. "Let's go. I have an idea," Alex smiled and hugged Ryle. The two boys ran to the field and there was Aisha with Eleonora. Eleonora ran up to Alex and stood near him. Ryle hugged Aisha "We need to do something about it. We can't lose him under any circumstance," Aisha said to the group. "It's about to be evening now, soon they will start," Eleonora worriedly said. "Won't anyone look for you? "Alex asked the girl. She looked down. Alex felt bad, was this the reason Skye didn't like staying home? Maybe this was why Eleonora was close to Skye. He was her only family. Silence took over until Ryle finally spoke. "I have an idea," he looked at everyone. "I trust the coach. We can go ask for his car and got to go the military place or camp whatever that is. If we are on time, we may manage to get him out before he is admitted." The plan was smart and well thought. But how will we know where the camp is?" Alex wondered. "There is one right outside of the town. It's surely that one," Aisha looked up and smiled. "It's a plan," Eleonora finally cheered up. The teens got ready and headed towards the coach's house.

Mission Rescue

They reached the coach's house. They just stood there, waiting for something to happen. Ryle let out a sigh. "I am going to talk to him. Hopefully, he will listen to me," Ryle walked to the door and rang the bell. The side door locked open. The coach was surprised to see Ryle "Hey buddy, what's up?" The coach had a worried look on his face. "Sir, we need your help," Ryle hesitated. "Tell me," he replied in a fairly deep tone. It sent shivers down Rye's spine. He took a deep breath and gained the confidence to speak. He had to do it for his best friend. He looked at the coach. "Skye is in trouble, and I can't explain why," the lad muttered. "We need your car to go and bring him back. We have no one else to turn to, sir please help us." The boy looked at him with pleading eyes. The coach was confused by Ryle's behavior. He knew that Ryle would not do anything bad. How could the Coach agree to something he did not know was going on? The coach let out a sigh and closed the door. Ryle pressed his lips together and punched the wall. "Shit!" he yelled out. The lad was frustrated that he could not manage to find a way and his only idea was wasted.

The door suddenly opened, and the coach stepped out. He picked up Ryle's hand and put his car keys in his palm "I don't know what you boys are up to," he glared at Alex. "And I hope it's nothing bad. If Skye is in trouble go, bring him back. We need him. Good luck," he pat Ryle's back. Everyone hugged the coach as he chuckled." Bring him back Ryle, I trust you," he whispered in the lad's ears. Ryle nodded as now he was determined. "Everyone in the car, now!" Ryle said and everyone ran to the car. Aisha sat in front as Alex stayed in the back seat with Eleonora. "I will bring everyone back safely, I promise." The coach had a proud smile. Ryle got in the driver's seat and twisted the key.

The drive started. Ryle knew how to drive but had no license. It was illegal and dangerous but the only thing they cared about was Skye. The road till one point was smooth but soon the anxiety in them rose. "They must have started by now," Elenora said while checking the time. "Don't worry, we will manage," Alex tried comforting her. Suddenly they heard someone snoring softly. "Who slept?" Eleonora giggled. "Aisha fell asleep," Ryle chuckled as the girl was asleep leaning on his shoulder. "I urge you guys to do the same. It's long drive," Ryle drove on a steady pace. "It's hard for me to sleep in cars," Eleonora mumbled. She felt awkward between them. She felt a bit like a burden. The girl looked down, picking her skin "just like her brother", Alex thought and chuckled. The lad went to the corner of the car leaning his back towards the door. "Eleonora put your legs on top of the back seat and lean your head on my chest. You will feel comfortable and be able to sleep," the lad winked at the younger girl. She looked at him with wide eyes, "Are you sure?" Alex nodded. The girl leaned on his chest as he caressed her hair. Soon she fell asleep too. Alex was sweet with her as she was Skye's younger sister. She acted exactly like her big brother. It was true that Skye had, in fact, raised her. "Thank you for helping me

Ryle. Without you, I wouldn't be able to help Skye," the boy muttered while caressing the sleeping girl's hair. Alex was grateful for everything but this time he knew Ryle deserved it. "Skye to not just your boyfriend but my best friend too. Don't thank me for something I am obliged to do," Ryle smiled as the road continued.

The blonde lad held back his tears. He leaned on the car window looking out. He didn't get a chance to say goodbye to Alex, not even Eleonora, his sister. She knew there was no use crying. The lad closed his eyes. Tears rushed down like beautiful waterfalls. As much as he wanted, he couldn't stop his tears. Skye was afraid about the hell he would face there. Would he be able to see his forbidden love ever again or not? Skye cried as he let down a silent sob. His father could not care less. The only thing that mattered to him was his reputation that was now "ruined". "We are reaching in about an hour. Get ready to go to your new home," his father spoke for the first time in a while. Skye wanted to protest, to tell him to stop, to go back home but he didn't even try. The blonde just nodded. He was tired. The lad closed his eyes imagining he was with Alex and soon fell asleep.

The car came to a stop. All shot up looking around. "Did we reach?" the lad looked around." "No, I don't know why the car stopped," Ryle's voice was filled with panic. He shook Aisha softly. "What's wrong?" she mumbled, still a bit sleepy. "Get down with me, the car is not moving," Ryle said as he stepped out. Aisha glanced back at the sleeping and smiled softly as she followed Ryle. They looked around but everything seemed normal. "Check the tires" Ryle muttered as Aisha bent down to look around. The back left tire was punctured. "Fuck," Ryle mumbled. "He must have a spare in the back," Aisha said as she open the trunk of the car. Ryle took the heavy tire out and placed it on the ground. Aisha tried to remove the tire but it was too heavy. The material was old and the tires needed to be removed with a special machine. Ryle tried but the tire was not coming out. A while had passed Ryle and Aisha had still not come back. Alex caressed Eleonora's hair "Eleonora, wake up," he said, trying not to startle the girl. The blonde's eyes opened. "They need us outside, let's go" Alex muttered as they both got out. "Ryle what's wrong? Alex said confused. "The tire is punctured though we a tried to change it, it's not coming out," Aisha replied as Ryle tried to pull the tire out. Eleonora teared up. "At this rate we will never reach on time," she held Alex's shirt. Alex noticed the girl's pain in her eyes as he bent down to her level. "I told you, you need to be strong. Don't worry I am here," he patted her head and went to Ryle. "On the Count of three, pull it." Alex held the car. "One two....... three!" the lad put all his energy and picked the car up. Ryle quickly pulled the tire out. Aisha cheered as she hugged Eleonora. "Until we are here, you don't need to worry". She patted the girl's back. Soon, they were back on the road. Ryle tried to speed but they still were delayed because of the tire incident. Eleonora teared up as she hugged Alex. "Guys another 15 minutes," Ryle tried to give them strength.

They had finally reached. The blonde got out with his father holding his bags. Skye didn't want to seem weak, so he did not shed tears. They walked inside as a tall man greeted Skye. His father seemed friends with that man, so it was an instinct that Skye did not like him. The blonde remained silent. He nodded to everything. The tall man was a headmaster or that's what Skye took him for. "This is your new dorm where you are going to stay," the man said in a commanding voice. The lad nodded; he hated it. The rest of the boys seemed bulky and strong. Far from what Skye was. The blonde gulped; he did not like it. His father smirked. Fucking tyrant. The tall man left with his father trapping the boy in the hell hole. Not even a goodbye. That's how much his father cared.

They had finally reached. Alex quickly hopped out of the car. He noticed some black car he saw almost every night, Skye and Alex took a deep breath trying not to panic. Ryle got out, as he analyzed the situation. Skye was gone. Alex ran his hand through his hair. Ryle sighed, there was nothing he could do now. He patted the boy's back. Alex sighed as he knew that his lover was long gone now. Ryle suddenly grabbed Alex's arm and hid him behind the car. The two boys watched as the monster went to his car and soon drove off. Alex's palm grew into a fist. "I will kill that man," the lad murmured. Ryle patted his back from him. "Go talk to the child, she needs you," so he forced out a weak smile. Alex nodded getting inside the car. "Hey sweetheart," he tried to be soft with the girl who had already pooled tears in her eyes. "He's gone, isn't he?" she whimpered as the tears got harder to control. Alex looked at the girl and closed his eyes before nodding. Eleonora clung onto Alex sobbing her heart out. She had lost her brother, her family, her everything. The girl cried thinking about all the moments they spent together. No one would save her from nightmares anymore. No one would save her from nightmares anymore, no one would cuddle her, hold her, love her….. She cried her heart out on Alex's chest. She blamed herself for not taking care of him but now it is too late. Too late for regrets.

The lad sat on his bed still in shock. He felt so unsafe. His heartbeat started to race. Now there was no one to make him feel safe. His biological family just made it worse, "Am I that bad? Do I deserve it? Who will take care of me now?" the lad was finally alone. He looked down, his hands trembled. Flashes of his traumatic past flashed before his eyes. He could not feel vulnerable. Everyone seemed like an enemy. Tears dwelled in his eyes. He just wanted to feel safe, secure, loved but I guess his fate did not have that in store for him. He wished he would change, he wished he was gone. Panic took over him. No one could make him feel safe. He felt all alone. The boy's family did not seem related they just used to be random bodies or entities living under the same roof. The lad held his knees close to his chest. The boy trembled. All he needed was self-confidence. Someone to rely on but…..He looked out of the distant window. Maybe somewhere far away, people are happy. They deserve it. I do not, apparently. He let his tears fall. "I wish everything changed that's where my happy ending ended did not it…?""

In Time

Time had slipped out of their hands. The three teenagers sat numbly. The blonde girl lay motionless on Alex's chest. She was sound asleep, exhausted from the endless tears that had soaked her rosy cheeks. Alex was grateful that she had fallen asleep; it was better than being awake with immense pain. Sometimes, sleep is your only escape from this cruel world, from this cruel reality. Aisha snuggled up close in Ryle's arms as silent tears rolled down her cheeks. Ryle bit his lower lip holding back tears as he caressed his lover's arms. He felt broken, like there was nothing else he could do about it, Alex dug his nails into his palms, feeling enraged Not at anyone but at himself. He could not help but blame himself for the situation. He hated himself for it. Even if he did, even if he was guilty, even if he regretted his actions nothing could be changed now. The stars stopped twinkling, the moon stopped twinkling, the moon stopped shining as the night just grew darker, A tear escaped Alex's eye as he let out a deep sigh.

The two boys had sneaked out as usual. It was in the middle of the night when they had decided to meet up. The only time they felt safe. Skye held Alex's hand and he let out a soft giggle as he ran in front. Alex admired his lover, his giggle as he was running in front. Alex admired his lover, his godly eyes even shone in the darkness. They were the light of Alex's life, they went to their usual spot, the school field. The forbidden lovers lay beside each other admiring the beauty of the night. Alex held Skye by the waist and pulled him closer as they kept each other warm on a cold night. Skye's blonde hair draped across his angelic face; his eyes rested as he kept his body close to Alex's. "Come close," Alex whispered in a husky voice. Skye obeyed and scooted closer to his lover. Alex squeezed the blonde into his chest. He never wanted to let go. Skye swiftly pulled himself away and looked into Alex's eyes. A moment of silence passed; the only thing that be heard was the crickets' chirps. "Will this ever end?" Skye blurted out of the blue. Alex was perplexed by the sudden question. He sat up straight and pulled the boy onto to his lap "I give you my word, I won't ever let it end. I won't ever let anything take you away from me, I promise." So many promises were made and look at them now, torn apart, separate, and all alone. Do promises always break? Alex planted a soft kiss on Skye's temple. "I have somewhere to take you," Alex said with a small glimmer in his eyes. "Where?" Skye chuckled as he stood up. After a long time, he had seen Alex excited about something. Alex was not exactly the type to get eager about anything. "It's a suprise," Alex held Skye's hand and led him deeper into the night. Skye had no idea where they were going but he never questioned Alex. Soon they reached a tall fence behind the fence laid a small park where only a couple used to go. A small smile crept up on Skye's face but that was short-lived; once he saw Alex climbing over the fence, Skye's eyes popped out. "You expect me to cross over that!?" Skye sat there shocked. "Unless you want to fly over it," Alex joked as he jumped down on the other side. "I can't," Skye said as he turned his back around "What do you mean you can't cross over,

Skye?" Alex started to get annoyed. Skye noticed the annoyance in his partner's voice and frowned softly. "I am too scared," he murmured. Alex got pissed off at that, and anger started taking over him. "Fine you stay, I am out of here," Alex said aggressively and stormed inside the park on his own. Skye was left all alone in the middle of the night. The blonde teared up. He hated it when Alex got mad. When Alex was enraged, he was like a bull who only saw red. Skye started to panic. What was he supposed to do now? He saw Alex storming towards him and freaked out. His legs tremble. Alex jumped over the fence and went up to Skye. Alex was silent as he picked up Skye in his arms. "Hold onto me," he demanded and Skye quickly obeyed. He had no idea what was going on. The boy held tightly onto the man he loved and admired. Alex gave him a feeling of comfort and safety. Nothing could hurt him when Alex was around, Alex was strong he climbed the fence with Skye holding onto him, and soon jumped down. Alex looked at Skye. He touched Skye's legs to make sure he wasn't hurt. "I am fine, Alex," Skye mumbled with a sweet smile. "I won't let anything hurt you, ever. The day I do, I have failed in life. I have failed my love," Alex passionately kissed the boy in his arms.

"I can't let anything hurt him" Alex jotted up. His body couldn't physically accept that he could lose Skye. At this point, it didn't matter if he wanted Skye. He needed him. He could not live without him. That was a fact that no matter how much he denied it was true. "What do you think you can do now? It's too late," Ryle looked away. "Don't you dare say that!" Alex gritted his teeth. "Even if I have to make the stars and moon collide to bring him back, I will." "Fighting is of no use," Aisha wiped away her now dried tears and looked at them, "You will wake Eleonora up. We must think of something". Aisha looked at the window. Everyone started to think. Life without Skye was not an option for them. Elenora was up now. She lay in Alex's arms trying to help in any way possible. She could not sit around while her only family could potentially be taken apart from her. The world stopped for a second. Aisha gasped softly. "I have an Idea," she smirked.

Escape

Everyone sat up straight. They all gathered up around Aisha, "Listen up," she said. "Me, Alex, and Ryle can sneak. Potentially find Skye and try our best to get out of there." She bit her inner cheek and looked at the others waiting for a response. "It's not that easy, Aisha, they have cameras everywhere. Most likely alarms too. Plus, we do not even know where they have kept Skye," Ryle said analyzing the idea. It was not bad, but they could not risk being caught here. Leave them. Skye would get into a lot of trouble in case they were caught. Alex looked away frustrated, trying not to lose hope. "That would not be a problem," Elenora looked at them. It caught everyone off guard. How could she say that it was not that easy? Eleonora kept looking at them as she understood they were confused, and she had to give an explanation. "I can hack into the site and find where Skye is. Freezing the cameras won't be hand," she explained. "What about the alarms?" Alex questioned. "Now that's tricky but for 20 minutes at max, I can shut them off." Everyone froze. They were speechless and just did not know what to say, "How do you know all that?" Aisha wondered. "I have done my fair share of research I like getting involved in this stuff," Eleonora said like it was nothing. The teens were impressed, "What about the guards though?" Aisha looked at the boys. Ryle smiled "We can take care of that can't we Alex?" Alex gave a proud smile and nodded. Elenora took out her phone and got to work. The clicks on her phone were quick and swift she knew what she was doing. The teens admired her. Eleonora knew she would get into a lot of trouble. But she was willing to go to any extent for her brother. She stopped and looked at the others, "Skye is in room 8E, meaning he is on the eighth floor in the fifth room. Seeing the institute's map here there is a back room on the left side with easy access to the staircase. It is patrolled by 2 guards. If you manage to knock them out, you will be fine. "Don't stress about that" Alex pat her back. The three teens got up and started to prepare for their departure. Eleonora searched her pockets and took out 4 small earphones as she handed them to the others and wore one herself. "Keep this we can communicate," she smiled. "How do you have this?" Alex was amazed. "I just do," she spoke. "She is way cooler than Skye," Ryle said amazed. Alex and Aisha glared at him. "Okay okay, sorry!" Ryle raised his hand innocently as Eleonora giggled. Eleonora looked back at her phone and clicked. "The cameras are frozen." "What are we waiting for then? Let's go," Aisha said as the others nodded. "Just remember you have 20 minutes before the alarms get back on. Be quick," Eleonora warned as everyone geared up. "It's risky." she said. "I am willing to put my life on line for him. I would die for him. This is the least I can do," Alex replied. Elenora smiled. Aisha took the lead as they started to leave. Alex leaned closer to Eleonora's ear "Your brother is proud of you," he whispered and left. Eleonora teared up. But quickly wiped her tears. She clicked a final time on her phone and the alarms were disarmed. "The clock is ticking," she whispered on the earpiece.

The teens hid in the darkness of the night as they started getting closer. The wind blew and the leaves rustled in the depth of the night, nothing could be seen. Ryle noticed a light. "See that? It's probably the back door," he whispered. They hid behind some bushes and started getting closer. They stayed hidden waiting for the right moment to jump out. "Be careful, the guards are specifically trained. Don't get yourself hurt," Eleonora spoke through the earpiece. "On the count of three," Alex whispered "One.... Two.... Snap!" Aisha stepped on a twig as the guards immediately looked towards them. "Oh fuck," Ryle said as at once he and Alex jumped out and lunged on the other two. Aisha was startled by the suddenness but ran to help too. The fight was on Ryle punched the guard in the jaw only to receive one on his stomach in return. Alex had to fight with the tougher one. He tried to fight but kept receiving blows. Aisha stepped in and punched the guy on his chest making his body jerk. "Need help, I see," she smirked at Alex. "Maybe," he chuckled. The fight kept going back and forth. At least no sounds could be heard except occasional grunts and groans. Three of them started to get covered in bruises but they did not care less about the pain. It was all worth it. "Guys, the clock is ticking be quick we are running out of time," Eleonora spoke once again. Alex looked at the others as his heart started to race. Aisha kicked the guy on the calf making him fall. "Run, go get Skye can handle this," Ryle punched the other guy down, Alex nodded. "Thanks," he mumbled as he rushed to the door.

Alex went in to find dimly lit stairs. "Which room did you say again El?" He started to run up the stairs. "8E, eighth floor the fifth room. Be quick please time is running out," Eleonora started to panic a bit, "Don't worry we got this." Alex increased his speed. Despite his efforts, the staircase seemed like it would never end. The light did not help him either. The lad counted the floors in his mind and made sure not to miss any. His brain was a ruckus at this point. The goal was one. Take Skye and get out of there. Soon he reached the eighth floor. His heart pounded in his chest. He could feel his heart in his throat. "8E,8E,8E" he mumbled looking around the rooms. He stood in front of this big door. "8E" was written on the top. The lad entered the room as quietly as possible. He looked around but there was no sign of Skye. His hands were shaking. "Are you sure he is in 8E?" His words were shaky. "Yes, Alex! I cannot be wrong in this," Eleonora responded instantly. Alex was about to lose all his hope when he heard a sniffling sound from the corner of the room. Alex quickly looked at the corner. There he was, Skye, his love, his life.

Alex walked over to him. His heart clenched; with every step he took, the pace of his heartbeat increased. Skye looked at him and immediately realized who he was. Even though the room was dark, no matter where he was he would always recognize his lover. "A...Alex?" he refused to believe what was in front of him. Time slowed down, no one moved, only their breaths could be heard. For the first time they did not lunge to hug each other, they just stayed there frozen looking into each other's eyes. Alex teared up at the sight of his boy, how could he ever live without him? He couldn't control himself. He picked up Skye and pressed him up against him as both shed tears. "I will always protect you, I promise," they passionately attached their lips. Some promises are never broken, they are kept and cherished.

Alex quickly broke the kiss and looked at Skye. "We need to get you out of here quick!" he held Skye's arm tightly as he led him out of the room. Skye just followed Alex. His savior had come to the rescue. They rushed down the stairs. Alex ran too fast; Skye could not keep up. "I cannot run this fast," the lad whimpered Alex sighed as he stopped and picked Skye up bridal style. "I got you," Alex started to run down the stairs. They rushed, went as quickly as they could. "Where are they?" Aisha started getting worried. "They will be here anytime now..." Ryle consoled him. They had knocked down the guards and it did not seem like they would wake up anytime soon. "Guys! You have 20 seconds... I don't know what happened, I thought we had more time but we didn't. I screwed up, get out of there quickly. The alarms will go back on," Eleonora panicked. There was no way they could make it. Alex ran as he held his boy close. Aisha and Ryle saw Alex "Quick come out! We have to go!" Ryle yelled. Skye was surprised on seeing them but had no time for words. Alex jumped out in a hurry. "Let's go," the teens smiled at each other. That's when the alarms went off. The teens had no time left. They all sprinted towards the car. More guards noticed them and ran in their direction to stop them. The car was in sight. Elenora opened all the doors as she saw them coming. The whole place was ringing as more alarms went off though they did not give a damn. Ryle was the first to reach as he sat and started the car. "In quick!" he yelled out. Aisha sat near him as Alex quickly shoved himself inside with Skye slamming the door. "Drive, Drive, Drive!" Aisha yelled.

A Smooth Ending

Ryle pressed as hard as he could on the accelerator, he swung the starting wheel with all his strength. They needed to get out of there as soon as possible. Aisha looked back and noticed three black cars following them, "Ryle please be quicker they will catch on to us," her breath was shaky as she spoke in a panic. "We need to lose them," Alex said still holding onto Skye tightly. Skye could not process what was going on. All of this felt surreal to him. Regardless of the state of trepidation, he was just glad that now he was safe, well almost. "Buckle up everyone, you are not going to like this," Ryle smirked. The black-haired boy hit the brakes out of nowhere, making everyone jolt forward. He paused for a moment before he quickly changed direction. The lad took an aggressive left turn into the woods. Honestly, he had no idea where he was headed;, all he cared about was getting those cars off his back. The car was at its full power. Ryle drove as if it was a racing car, he kept taking aggressive turns making everyone jump up from time to time. The youngest out of them tried to hold on to the car's handle as tight as she could but got hurt from time to time. The girl let out soft whimpers from time to time. Alex sat in the other corner of the car as Skye sat beside him. He held Skye's arm making sure he did not get hurt by the sudden jerks of the car. Skye soon noticed the distress his sister was in. He always noticed it at the end of the day he was the one who had raised her. Skye let go of Alex and briskly picked the girl up in his arms. "You are safe, your brother is here," he whispered into her ear with the sweetest most majestic voice. Eleonora latched onto him. Upon hearing his voice, all the muscles in her body relaxed. She took deep breaths as she laid her head on his chest. The girl could faintly hear her brother's heartbeat. She knew that she was safe. After 20 minutes of mindless driving, they were on the road home. Ryle stopped the car on the side to make sure everyone was ok. "Is everyone fine?" Silence filled up the car.

"You guys came," Skye's voice filled up the tranquility. Skye was grateful, he never expected to be rescued from that nightmare of a place and yet he was. "What did you expect from us? Sit around and watch you suffer? You are our friend Skye, we can't let any trouble come upon you," Ryle pat Skye on the back. "Let alone friend, you are our family. If you are in trouble, we are in trouble. we are in this together." Aisha smiled, pleased that Skye was finally back. Skye tried not to tear up. Words could not express how thankful he was feeling. "Without Eleonora, this would not be possible. She is the one who brought us all together," Alex winked at Eleonora praising her. Skye chucked and looked at his sister. "So, you are the mastermind behind this?" he caressed her hair. "Anything for you brother. I could not stand the thought of losing my only family," she spoke in tears. Skye bit his bottom lip as he hugged his sister tightly. "No more tears now. Let's go back and take some rest we need it," Aisha said to cheer up the mood. Everyone agreed. Indeed, they were all tried corpses at this point. Ryle softly started to drive them all home as they got some shut-eye. Sometimes all hope is not lost. No matter how bad things look they do get better. That night the teens slept all cuddled up in the car. It was cozy and safe for them, just some teenagers finding home and comfort in each other. That's all they needed.

In the morning, they all gathered up at Ryle's place. Ryle wanted to go and return the coach's car. He was grateful for the help he was given without that he knew that nothing could be possible. Aisha walked out of the room and looked at the two lovers sitting beside each other on the couch. She gave them a soft smile. "She is sound asleep, don't worry." She sat on the chair in front of them. "What do you plan on doing now? We got you out of there but what now?" Aisha sighed looking at Skye. "She's got a point where are you going to stay? And what if your bitch of a dad comes?" Alex's question worried his partner. Skye rested his elbows on his knees. "Honestly I have no idea, the top priority in my mind is keeping El safe". Skye did not know what to do, all he wanted was a place that he knew she was protected from any harm or danger "What's all the ruckus about?" Ryle walked into the room as he sat beside Aisha "Look who's back" Alex teased "Yeah, yeah now tell me," Ryle looked at Aisha. "We are trying to figure out where will Skye stay away from danger." She bit her inner cheek. Ryle raised his eyebrows. "He can stay with me, from the point that I live alone I don't mind," Ryle shrugged. "Eleonora can stay here too." Skye's eyes widened "Really!?" his breath hitched. Ryle smiled and nodded. "For a matter of fact, you all can stay over. We can divide the bills and chores" he laughed. Everyone was left amazed. "Sick bro, let's do it!" Alex cheered as the others laughed and agreed.

Their happiness was short-lived as soon as they heard loud bangs on the door. Skye gulped; he knew who it was. Alex got up in anger about to go and answer the door. Ryle held him back. "Let me" he walked up to the door and answered it. Skye's father stood there enraged. "Bring my son out!" he yelled. "I cannot sir. He does not want to and without his will, neither of us can force him," Ryle replied in a calm tone. "I don't care," the man responded. Ryle felt a bit taken aback not knowing what to say. Alex held Skye close to keep him from panicking. Aisha walked out with a devilish smile plastered on her face as she walked towards the angered man. She leaned close to his ear taking Ryle by surprise. "If you don't leave your kids alone, we will expose how you blackmail small industries into giving you money for your own profit. And trust me we got all the proof we need from your children so watch out." She pulled back. Aisha knew all of this because Skye had talked about it back when they were dating. The man knacked hissed. "Keep away from my business," he blurted out scared and hurried away from there. Satisfied, the teens came inside as now finally they were safe. Aisha stood at the balcony lost in her thoughts. "I wish I could turn back time.... I wish I was back to the days when someone cared about me or at least when I felt like someone did. I feel like no one ever cares and now everything has changed. Even while spending pleasant time with someone, it brings me back to those days. That scares me, will this moment go away? Will this end too? Will I lose them too?" Ryle stood near her, "Are you okay princess?" She nodded, unwilling to express her true emotions to him. They looked at the other boys playing in the garden. "Will all this end Ryle?" The girl looked into her lover's eyes in desperation of hearing words of comfort. He smiled, "Everything changes darling, we don't know whether it's going to be good or bad but that's the mystery of life, love". He pinched her nose as her eyebrows frowned. "I will always be with you, don't frown," he chuckled as he hugged her. "I will never let us break apart; that is the only thing that will remain I promise." He caressed her brown hair as tears filled her eyes. Tears of happiness not sadness. The girl looked up at him as he flashed his charming smile. The comforting sound and actions were finally her to own. They were theirs. She smiled, "I am happy." It's a normal phase but for her it meant the world. More than her it meant everything to him. He cupped her cheeks. Her soft skin rested against his palm. Life could not be more beautiful. Their lips touched as they were finally together.... finally, one. I guess it is true, time changes everything good or bad. All you got to do is keep holding on....

ABOUT THE AUTHOR

Name: Konstantina Priyadarshini Vasileiadou

Age: 14

Nationality: Greek & Indian

*K*onstantina Priyadarshini Vasileiadou, a 14-year-old literary prodigy, possesses a unique blend of Indian and Greek heritage that serves as a canvas for her imaginative storytelling. Born to an Indian mother and a Greek father, Konstantina is a maiden writer whose pen weaves tales of teenage romance, creating narratives that resonate with the hearts of young readers.

In her debut work, a captivating teenage romantic fiction, Konstantina brings to life the universal experiences of adolescence, love, and self-discovery. Drawing inspiration from the colourful tapestry of her dual cultural upbringing, her writing effortlessly blends the spices of Indian romance with the poetic allure of

Greek passion. The result is a narrative that not only explores the complexities of young love but also introduces readers to the enchanting fusion of Eastern and Western traditions.

Konstantina's storytelling prowess goes beyond the printed page. Through her characters and plotlines, she explores themes of cultural identity, family dynamics, and the transformative power of love. Her ability to infuse her work with the warmth of Indian familial bonds and the picturesque landscape of Greek romance creates a truly immersive reading experience.

As a young writer, Konstantina is not only shaping her literary voice but also acting as a cultural bridge between India and Greece. Her stories resonate with readers across borders, celebrating the shared emotions that connect us all, regardless of cultural background.

Balancing her creative pursuits with the demands of adolescence, Konstantina remains a dedicated student maintaining a balance between her academic studies and her passion for writing. Her commitment to education reflects her belief that knowledge is a powerful tool for breaking down barriers and building bridges between cultures. Her academic journey contributes depth and insight to her writing, reflecting a thoughtful and well-rounded approach to storytelling. Her commitment to learning serves as a foundation for her storytelling, adding depth and insight to her narratives.

Konstantina Priyadarshini Vasileiadou, is not only a promising young author but also a cultural ambassador whose words carry the spirit of two nations. As she continues to explore the realms of teenage romance and beyond, Konstantina is poised to make a significant impact on the literary world, captivating hearts with her stories and fostering understanding through the magic of love and culture.

www.ingramcontent.com/pod-product-compliance
Lightning Source LLC
LaVergne TN
LVHW041851070526
838199LV00045BB/1540